英语满分训练

中考英语

阅读理解专项训练

★ 把握命题趋势　体现热点题型
★ 材料原汁原味　练考融会贯通
★ 考前热身自测　助你冲刺满分

总 主 编　黄　侃
分册主编　方　星
编　　委　赵叶丽　刘　瑶　郑　慧
　　　　　徐　蓉　杨　宁　何礼荣
　　　　　江　静　陈亚兰

南京大学出版社

前　　言

　　全日制义务教育《英语课程标准》明确指出,初中三个年级(即七年级到九年级)的学生除英语教材外,课外阅读量应分别达到 4 万词以上、10 万词以上以及 15 万词以上。由此可见,"课标"对初中学生的英语阅读能力提出了较高要求。中考阅读由"完形填空、阅读短文和首字母填空"三大"板块"组成,占全卷(96 分)的 50 分。阅读理解题既考查学生综合运用英语的能力,也考查学生运用英语解决实际问题的能力。它是能力题也是拉分题。学生们只有通过分类阅读,熟悉不同体裁文章的结构特点和设题手法,增加生活常识,关注热点事件,注重学科间综合知识积累,掌握阅读规律,才能达到理解语境、强化语篇和跨文化意识的目的,迅速提高阅读能力。

一、中考英语阅读题型

　　中考阅读理解题型可分为:客观阅读理解和主观阅读理解。客观阅读理解是指读完一篇短文后就文后的几个问题作出正确的选择,可分为单选题(Choose the right answer)和判断句子正误 (True or False) 两种类型。主观阅读理解是指读完一篇短文后,根据短文内容,按要求完成任务。这些任务包括:回答问题(一般疑问句、特殊疑问句、选择疑问句或反义疑问句)、完成句子、中英互译、连词成句、正误判断、多项选择、排列顺序、短语匹配、图表填充等等。

二、中考英语阅读内容

　　中考阅读理解文章题材广泛,内容丰富,设题灵活,既考查学生的词汇、句法、日常交际用语,又考查学生对欧美文化的知晓程度。文章内容涉及社会文化、日常生活、科普知识、人物传记、历史、地理、体育、音乐等,体裁包括记叙文、说明文、议论文、应用文等。

三、中考阅读技巧

　　阅读短文是读者利用自己的语言知识和背景知识对文章所进行的一种积极的思维过程。阅读短文应遵循由整体到细节的原则,按"全文、段落、句子、词语"的步骤阅读文章。可采用通读、细读和复读的方法找到最佳答案。在通读、细读和复读中,复读尤为重要且行之有效。通过复读来审视、推敲答案,提高答题命中率。

　　1. 短文——问题——短文(Passage—Question—Passage)

　　针对记叙文、说明文和议论文中所设计的全局性问题,学生们可先读文章,然后再根据问题查阅文章,最后解答问题。其特点是:有利于学生把握文章的主旨和作者的态度,有利于解答全局性问题、推理判断和词义猜测等深层次问题。这种方法可能耗时多,学生们在阅读时难以把握考查的重点。

2. 问题——短文——问题(Question—Passage—Question)

针对应用文中所出现的细节问题,学生们要先看问题,然后再带着问题去阅读文章。阅读时要把注意力放在与问题直接相关的关键词语上,一旦找到所需要的信息,就立即停止扫描式的阅读,然后仔细地阅读相关部分后答题。其特点是:针对性强,节省时间,可以用来解答事实性和细节性的问题,但是对解答主旨性和推理性的问题效果不佳。

3. 阅读——寻找——变换——检查(Read—Search—Change—Check)

针对以任务型阅读为主体的主观阅读题(填写表格),学生们首先要认真阅读文章,找到关键词或关键句。其次,要注意句式的变化,学会使用"换一种说法"。再次,如果在文中找不到直接答案时,要学会用自己的语言组织句子。最后,要通过复读,查漏补缺。

本书根据中考阅读要求、命题原则和命题趋势,通过对人物类、体育类、科普类、应用类和说明类文章的分析,介绍客观阅读和主观阅读文章的设题原则和应试策略,同时还为学生们提供了一百多篇富有时代气息,体现时代精神,贴近学生生活,有助于了解英语国家文化,提高人文素养的主、客观阅读文章供大家进行实战演练。

在非英语环境中学习英语,阅读是最主要的手段。根据阅读的目的,我们可以把阅读分为语言应用性阅读和语言学习性阅读。语言应用性阅读以获取知识和信息为主要目的,而语言学习性阅读则以通过阅读逐步提高英语语言水平为主要目的。掌握语言知识(指语音、语法、词汇)和发展语言能力(指听、说、读、写)是互相促进,相辅相成的。因此,只有增加了语言知识,才能为大量的阅读铺平道路。而在阅读实践中所培养起来的语感和处理英语语句的技巧又可以增进阅读理解的准确性,促进英语语言水平的提高。学生们只有在平时注重阅读,巧用阅读技巧,才能提高阅读能力。

黄 侃

2009 年 6 月于南京

目　　录

第一部分 客观阅读理解

客观阅读理解是指读完一篇短文后就文后的几个问题做出正确的选择,可分为单选题(Choose the right answer)和判断句子正误(True or False)两种类型。客观阅读理解的文章所涉及的内容丰富,题材多样,这对于我们正确答题提出了较高的要求。在练习与考试中,我们可以注意以下几条客观阅读的解题技巧:

1. 标题往往体现了文章的大意,会给我们一些提示。通过标题,我们可以推测文章的大致内容,这也有利于对文章的理解,更重要的是能提高我们做题的效率。因此,文章如果有标题,一定要认真阅读。

2. 一般情况下可采用"倒读法"。即先看问题,然后带着问题去读短文,边读边捕捉文中与问题相关的信息点,这样针对性更强,可以节省时间,提高效率。当然,如果文章较短,则可以采用"顺读法",即先看短文,然后再去看题。

3. 快速阅读全文,掌握大意。认真分析一下题材和体裁。如果是记叙文,应尽快把握文章中的五个"w"(who, where, when, what, why)和一个"h"(how)。掌握了这些,就等于抓住了整个事件的全部过程;如果是说明文,则必须理解文中说明的事物的本质;如果是关于地理、旅游、文化等方面的文章,则要重点了解各种信息之间的关系。

4. 对于比较简单的题目,往往只要通读全文,就可以从文章中直接找到答案。在做题时首先要确保这些题目"一次成功"。有些题目要求对文中的个别生词或关键词作出解释。解这类题要充分理解上下文之后才能作答。还有些题不能从文中直接找到答案,必须对文章内容进行逻辑推理后才能得到正确答案。这就需要我们具备各方面的知识,仔细琢磨。此外,另一些题是考查文章的中心、标题或某一段的大意等。我们如果想正确作答,就要善于发现文章的主题句和主题词,然后通过分析和推理找出答案。

5. 扩大词汇量,巧猜生词。在阅读理解中遇到生词是很自然的现象。阅读中我们可以:(1) 利用构词法知识猜测词义。如常见的-er,-or, -tion, un-, im-, in-, dis-等。(2) 利用上下文的相关信息猜测词义。如同位语关系、反义关系、因果关系等等。(3) 运用常识猜测词义。此外,在平时的学习中,我们还应注意不断地扩大词汇量。可以运用归纳法,把同一类别的词汇归纳在一起,并不断进行补充记忆。比如,把有关体育运动的词汇、学校生活的词汇归纳在一起记忆。

6. 纠正不良阅读习惯,提高阅读速度。由于阅读理解的阅读量一般都较大,因此提高阅读速度是至关重要的。为了达到快速阅读的目的,一定要做到不出声地阅读,减少返读或回视,不要长时间地停留在某一个生词上,更不能逐字逐句将英文翻译成中文再去理解。

7. 拓宽知识面,增加背景知识。阅读理解的短文所涉及的背景知识题材多样,内容广泛,包括天文地理、风土人情、政治历史、文化教育、科学技术、交通环境、人物传略等等。要力争使自己在各个方面都懂得一些,这样有利于更快更好地理解文章。

8. 避免以下四点不利因素的干扰:一、心理紧张。做题时要充满自信、沉着冷静。遇到难题时如果情绪紧张,只会越读越糊涂。二、不带着问题去阅读。对于较长的文章,如果不提前了解问题,一上来就盲目的阅读,只会白白浪费时间。三、仅凭主观印象和常识去答题。做阅读理解题时要严格按照本篇文章的内容来回答问题,而不能只凭自己的常识来判断答案。四、草率答题。有些试题干扰性极强,答案似是而非,我们一定要反复推敲,不能草率答题。

下面就让我们针对客观阅读的几种常见类型来练一练吧。

人物类

范文解析

Madame Curie was one of the greatest scientists in the world. She was born in Poland in 1867. She and her husband Professor Curie had a lab of their own. They spent a lot of time in their lab and made a great discovery. Together they won the Nobel Prize in physics and Madame Curie herself won the Nobel Prize in chemistry later.

True or False：

(　　) 1. Madame Curie and Professor Curie were brother and sister.

(　　) 2. Madame Curie was the greatest scientist in the world.

(　　) 3. Professor Curie won the Nobel Prize in physics with Madame Curie.

(　　) 4. Later they won the Nobel Prize in chemistry by themselves.

(　　) 5. Madame Curie was good at chemistry and physics.

【答案与解析】

1. F　可由文中第二行 "She and her husband Professor Curie…" 得知。关键是要明白 "husband" 一词的意思,从而可知二人是夫妻关系,而非兄妹或姐弟关系。

2. F　相应信息在文中第一句 "Madame Curie was one of the greatest scientists in the world." 要注意把握关键词组 "one of the greatest scientists",意思是世界上最伟大的科学家其中之一。而在第2题的句子中少了 "one of" 这个关键部分,从而导致意思与原文有差别。

3. T　相应信息在文中第三行 "Together they won the Nobel Prize in physics" 得知。其中的 they 就是指他们夫妻二人,所以是二人共同获得诺贝尔物理奖。

4. F　可由文中最后一句 "… and Madame Curie herself won the Nobel Prize in chemistry later." 得知。说明了之后居里夫人一个人获得了诺贝尔化学奖。而第4题的

句子中提到"they won ...",这显然不对。

5. **T** 这可以在读完全文后得知。居里夫人与丈夫一同获得诺贝尔物理奖,又在之后独自获得诺贝尔化学奖,说明她在这两个学科上都很擅长。

实战演练

1

Stones is an American high-jumper. He is 1.95 metres tall. When he was nine years old, he was watching TV one night. On the TV, he saw Brumel, the Russian high-jumper, broke the world record. He jumped 2.28 metres. The next day, Stones started jumping.

After four months, Stones jumped 1.50 metres. Now he is not young, but he still practises jumping for recreation.

True or False:

( ) 1. Stones wanted to be a high-jumper at the age of fourteen.

( ) 2. Brumel broke the world record.

( ) 3. Stones jumped 2.28 metres.

( ) 4. Stones jumped 1.50 metres eight years later.

( ) 5. Stones has stopped training now.

2

Einstein(爱因斯坦) was born in 1879 in Germany. As a child, he was slow to talk. But when he was fourteen years old, he became clever. He taught himself maths from textbooks. He studied hard because he wanted to be a physicist.

In 1901, Einstein began teaching. In 1902 he went on with his study at the University of Zurich. Several years later, he put forward his famous Theory of Relativity(相对论).

To most people the Theory of Relativity is hard to explain. But once Einstein explained it very well to a group of young students. He said, "When you sit with a good girl for two hours, you think it is only a minute. But when you sit on a hot fire for a minute, you think it's two hours. That is relativity."

Later Einstein went to America and never left there. In 1955, Einstein's life ended at the age of seventy-six.

True or False：

(   ) 1. Einstein was born in 1901.

(   ) 2. Einstein was very clever when he was a child.

(   ) 3. Einstein wanted to be a physicist.

(   ) 4. Einstein put forward the Theory of Relativity.

(   ) 5. Einstein died in America at the age of seventy-six.

3

Thomas Edison was a great inventor. One day, about one hundred years ago, he stood by a strange-looking machine. He said the words, "Mary had a little lamb." Then something marvelous happened—the machine talked back. He had invented phonograph (留声机).

The machine, however, did not work very well. Another famous inventor, Alexander Graham Bell, helped to improve it. People were not sure whether they liked listening to the phonograph. Then a great singer, Emrico Caruso, made some records. Everyone loved them, and the phonograph became popular.

Today we can listen to our favourite singers whenever we want to. Thanks to Thomas Edison.

Choose the right answer：

(   ) 1. Thomas Edison called his "talking machine" a _____.

    A. photograph   B. phonograph   C. record player D. telephone

(   ) 2. The name of the great singer was _____.

    A. Thomas Edison   B. Alexander Graham Bell

    C. Emrico Caruso   D. Mary Smith

(   ) 3. Sometimes even an inventor needs _____.

    A. more money   B. less time

    C. thanks   D. help

(   ) 4. The word "marvelous" means _____.

    A. wonderful   B. usual   C. bad   D. popular

(   ) 5. The best title of this passage is _____.

    A. Alexander Graham Bell

    B. The Invention of the Phonograph

    C. Inventors always help each other

    D. How Emrico Caruso Made Records

4

Yao Ming, the center of the Chinese National Men's Basketball Team, served the

Houston Rockets in the 2002 NBA. The 2. 26m 120kg center becomes the first one which comes from a foreign team. Yao Ming was born in Shanghai in September,1980. His mother was a center and captain of the Chinese National Women's Team. His father played basketball，too. Yao Ming is widely known in China. He came to be a very important basketball player in China Basketball Association(联赛). It's short for CBA. During the 2000~2001 season，he got 27. 1 scores.

For the Shanghai Oriental(东方) Sharks in every match，Yao Ming joined the Houston Rockets in November，2002. He said it was a new start in his basketball life. He would do his best to learn from the NBA and improve himself. Sport analyst(分析家) Bill Walton said, "Yao Ming has the potential(潜力)，and the capability(能力) of changing the future of basketball. "

Choose the right answer：

(   ) 1. The Houston Rockets is the name of a _____ team.

        A. table tennis   B. volleyball   C. basketball   D. golf

(   ) 2. Both Yao Ming's father and mother were _____.

        A. football players

        B. basketball players

        C. the center of the Chinese National Team

        D. the captains of the Chinese National Team

(   ) 3. Yao Ming _____ in CBA during the 2000~2001 season.

        A. does well   B. is fine   C. was fine   D. did well

(   ) 4. Yao Ming _____ the Houston Rockets in November，2002.

        A. did his best to join

        B. was well-known in

        C. became a member of

        D. left

(   ) 5. Sport analyst Bill Walton thought Yao Ming was able to _____.

        A. learn from the NBA

        B. change the future of basketball

        C. improve himself

        D. become the captain of the Houston Rockets

5

Bill Clinton took office on January 20th，1993 and became the 42nd USA president. He is the first president who was born after World War Ⅱ. He is also one of the youngest of all USA presidents. Clinton was born in a poor family in 1946. Three months before he was born，his father William Blats died. When he was small，his mother remarried Norger Clinton, so the boy's family name changed.

In the summer of 1963, Clinton won a drama contest(戏剧比赛), so he was given a chance to visit the city of Washington. During his visit he met President Kennedy in the White House. From that time on, he made up his mind to become a president.

Choose the right answer:

(　　) 1. How old was Clinton when he became the 42nd USA president?

　　A. About forty.　B. Over fifty.　　C. Forty-seven.　D. Thirty.

(　　) 2. Why was the boy's family name changed?

　　A. he became a president.　　　　　B. his family was poor.

　　C. his mother was ill.　　　　　　D. his mother remarried.

(　　) 3. In 1963 Clinton came to the City of Washington _____.

　　A. to take part in a drama contest　B. to have a talk with Kennedy

　　C. for a visit　　　　　　　　　　D. for his holiday

(　　) 4. What does the underlined phrase "took office" mean in the passage?

　　A. 拥有办公室　B. 带走办公室　　C. 就职　　　　D. 离开办公室

(　　) 5. This passage is about _____.

　　A. Bill Clinton　　　　　　　　　B. Norger Clinton

　　C. Kennedy　　　　　　　　　　　D. William Blats

6

Abraham Lincoln and John F Kennedy were presidents(总统) of the USA. Lincoln became president in 1861 and Kennedy became president in 1961. Both of them were shot(射中) in the head and killed. They were both shot on a Friday. Both of their wives were with them when they died. John Wilkes Booth, the man who shot Lincoln, was born in 1839. Booth was shot soon after he killed the president. The man who shot Kennedy was Lee Harvey Oswald. He was born in 1939 and was also shot soon after he killed the president. Lincoln had a secretary(秘书) called Kennedy. This secretary told him not to go out on the day he was shot. Kennedy had a secretary called Lincoln. This secretary told Kennedy not to go out on the day he was shot. The name of the man who became president after Lincoln was Johnson. The name of the man who became president after Kennedy was also Johnson. What a lot of coincidences(巧合)!

Choose the right answer:

(　　) 1. The main idea of this passage is about _____.

　　A. the presidents of the USA

　　B. the presidents's wives

　　C. two presidents who were killed in the USA

　　D. a sad story in the USA

(　　) 2. _____ shot President Lincoln.

      A. His secretary   B. Lee Harvey Oswald

      C. His wife   D. John Wilkes Booth

(　　) 3. Kennedy became president in _____.

      A. 1839   B. 1939   C. 1961   D. 1861

(　　) 4. What happened to both presidents on a Friday?

      A. They were born.

      B. They were shot.

      C. They didn't go out with their wives.

      D. They became presidents.

(　　) 5. Who were the two people called Johnson?

      A. The presidents' secretaries.

      B. The men who shot the presidents.

      C. The presidents' wives.

      D. The men who became presidents after Lincoln and Kennedy.

7

Alex Harley was born in the northeast of New York in 1921, but he spent most of his early life with his mother's family. Their history, his mother said, began with Toby. He was a slave from Africa and his name was Kintay.

Alex Harley went to school and then to college. In 1939, he joined the USA coastguard. As he was a black, his job was to wait on tables and wash dishes. In his spare time, he learned to write stories. He served in the coastguard for 20 years. After he retired he put all his time into writing.

Alex Harley remembered the stories his grandmother had told him. He began to study his family story. After a lot of research, Harley decided that Toby probably was Kinta Kinte for the West African on the Gambia River. He was sold as a slave in Annapolis, Maryland in 1767. Then Harley made a trip to Gambia and talked with a history expert in Juffure. The African historian made his conclusion stronger.

Alex Harley wanted to tell the experiences of black people in 18th-and-19th-century America. He spent 10 years researching and writing his family story for the book *Roots*. It was published in 1979. It won a special Pulitzer Prize. A few years later, a film series based on Harley's book was shown on American television.

True or False:

(　　) 1. Alex Harley was born in the northwest of New York in 1921.

(　　) 2. Alex Harley went to school and then to college.

(　　) 3. He often waited on tables and washed dishes only because of the colour of his skin.

(   ) 4. Harley made a trip to Gambia and talked with a physics expert in Juffure.

(   ) 5. He spent 10 years researching and writing his family story for the book *Roots*.

8

In 1964，Bruce Lee won the champion of America Karate(空手道) Competition in Florida. He was then only 24! Soon after the competition，three karate champions went to Lee's home together to challenge him along with a judo(柔道) champion，however，they all lost. There are many other stories about Bruce Lee. It was said that once when Lee was walking along the street of the China Town in Florida，he saw four hooligans were ragging(欺负) a Chinese girl. There were knives in their hands. Lee was very angry and put up a good fight with them，and he taught the hooligans a good lesson. The story spread quickly in America as well as the name Bruce Lee.

Lee was known as a famous film star，but he himself often said，"I'm first a man of Kung Fu fighter，then an actor." Lee went into the film trade just in order to make the Chinese Kung Fu known by the world. And he succeeded in doing so. The films such as Tang Shan Da Xiong and Game of Death were so popular that they are still on TV these days in China and other countries.

Lee got married to a girl called Linda，one of the Kung Fu fans in the year 1964. However，the marriage didn't last long because Lee died in the year 1973. He was only 33 at his death. Some people said he was murdered，but they didn't have any proof of that. He died of an accident by taking the wrong medicine which caused his death actually.

Choose the right answer：

(   ) 1. How many people went to challenge Bruce Lee after Lee won the Karate Champion?

     A. 1.   B. 2.   C. 3.   D. 4.

(   ) 2. What made Bruce Lee's name spread quickly in America?

     A. He has very wonderful Chinese Kung Fu.

     B. He attended some excellent films.

     C. He taught a lesson to the hooligans and saved a Chinese girl.

     D. He won the champion of American Karate Competition in Florida.

(   ) 3. Lee went into the film industry because _____.

     A. he was interested in acting

     B. he wanted to be famous

     C. he wanted to earn more money

D. he wanted to make Kung Fu known by the world

(　　) 4. How long did his marriage last?

    A. 5 years.   B. 7 years.

    C. 9 years.   D. 11 years.

(　　) 5. What was the cause for Lee's death?

    A. He was murdered.   B. He killed himself.

    C. He died of a car accident.   D. He took the wrong medicine.

9

Rebecca Stevens was the first woman to climb Mount Everest. Before she went up the highest mountain in the world, she was a journalist(记者) and lived in a small flat in south London.

In 1993, Rebecca left her job and her family and travelled to Asia with some other climbers. She found that life on Everest was hard. "You must carry everything on your back," she explained, "so you can only take things that you will need. You can't wash on the mountain, and in the end I didn't even take a toothbrush. I am usually a clean person but there is no water, only snow. Water is very heavy so you only take enough to drink."

When Rebecca reached the top of Mount Everest on May 17th, 1993, it was the best moment of her life. Suddenly she became famous.

Now she has written a book about the trip and people often ask her to talk about it. She has a new job, too, on a science programme on television.

Rebecca is well-known today and she has more money, but she still lives in the little flat in south London among her pictures and books about mountains!

Choose the right answer:

(　　) 1. Everest is a _____.

    A. country   B. mountain   C. company   D. magazine

(　　) 2. Rebecca went to Everest _____.

    A. alone   B. with her family

    C. with a climbing group   D. with her friends

(　　) 3. Rebecca didn't take too much luggage(行李) because she _____.

    A. didn't have many things   B. had a bad back

    C. had to carry it herself   D. there was no enough water

(　　) 4. Rebecca carried water for _____.

    A. drinking   B. cooking

    C. cleaning her teeth   D. washing

(　　) 5. After her trip, Rebecca _____.

A. earned the same money   B. stayed in the same flat
C. did the same job   D. wrote many books about the trip

10

Many young people in China know about Celine Dion, the famous French Canadian pop singer. She sang the song *My Heart Will Go On* for the movie *Titanic*. But do you know she had already become popular before that?

Celine Dion was born in a small town in Canada. She is the youngest child of the fourteen children in a musical family. Her parents and large family formed a singing group. They travelled and played folk music here and there. They were well-known in their home town. Celine's mother wrote the first song for her, and she recorded the song with her brother at the age of twelve. Rene Angelil, a local rock manager, was very interested in them. He asked Mrs Dion and her two children to come to his office. Later on he gave strong support to Celine. In 1994, Celine Dion got married to him.

As a singing star, Celine Dion received many prizes and soon became famous all over the world. She sang at the opening ceremony(开幕式) of the 1996 Olympic Games in Atlanta, USA. In 1997, she hit the whole world with the song *My Heart Will Go On*.

True or False:
(   ) 1. Celine Dion was born in a small town in France.
(   ) 2. Celine Dion wrote her first song by herself.
(   ) 3. In 1994, Celine Dion got married to Rene Angelil, a local rock manager who was very interested in her songs and gave strong support to her.
(   ) 4. Celine Dion didn't receive any prize until she sang the song *My Heart Will Go On*.
(   ) 5. Celine Dion sang at the opening ceremony of the 1996 Olympic Games in Atlanta, USA.

11

"I was in the bath at the time." Radcliffe says, "And my dad ran in and said, 'Guess who they have chosen to play the role of Harry Potter!' At that time I started to cry excitely. It was probably the happiest moment of my life."

Daniel Radcliffe was born on July 23rd, 1989 in England. He preferred to be called Danny. He wanted to be an actor when he was 5 years old, but his parents were not interested in the idea. However, Danny persuaded(说服) them and played his first major role in the BBC-TV play of *David Copperfield*(1999) in which he played the role of young David. Danny can also be seen in the movie *The Tailor of Panama*(2000), a spy thriller(惊险读物). But Danny was famous after the film of *Harry Potter*. The film came from the successful *Harry Potter* book series. According to the BBC，14 000 boys auditioned(面试) for the role. But the movie makers wanted a British boy to play the part of Harry，and director Chris Columbus wanted Danny for the role after seeing his performance in *David Copperfield*.

Choose the right answer：

(   ) 1. What was Radcliffe doing when he was told to play Harry Potter?

    A. He was doing his homework.

    B. He was reading on the balcony.

    C. He was taking a shower.

    D. He was watching TV.

(   ) 2. How old is Daniel Radcliffe now?

    A. 23.   B. 20.   C. 14.   D. 5.

(   ) 3. Why did Danny cry excitedly?

    A. Because he was chosen to play the leading role in *David Copperfield*.

    B. Because he was chosen to play the leading role in *The Tailor of Panama*.

    C. Because he was chosen to play the leading role in *Harry Potter*.

    D. Because his parents agreed his ideas of being an actor.

(   ) 4. How many boys auditioned for the role?

    A. 1 989.   B. 1 999.   C. 2 000.   D. 14 000.

(   ) 5. Why did the director choose Radcliffe to play the role of Harry Potter?

    A. Because he is a British boy.

    B. Because he is a well-known child actor.

    C. Because of his good acting in *David Copperfield*.

    D. Because of his smart appearance.

12

Wherever he appears，people will get shocked at the sight of him—a black colossus (巨人) or an iron tower.

At 2. 16 metres and 138 kilograms，he wears shoes size 57 that are like two boats. His hands are as large as two cattail leaf fans(蒲扇). He always shakes hands carefully and gently with the others for he is afraid his great strength may hurt them. He smiles gently so that his resonant voice won't frighten them. He even begins his chatting with shyness.

Shark O'Neal，who is 22 years old，has become a new NBA famous player and is a rising superstar or a "Black Horse". Now he has signed a seven-year contract valuing $40 million with the Orando Magics. In addition，he will get another huge amount of

$30 million from the advertisements all over the world. The NBA experts think he will be a billionaire at the age of 25, the highest record of its kind.

Shark O'Neal's mother is busy with answering and handling almost 1 000 letters a day which come mainly from his fans, while his father, Phillip, is in charge of O'Neal's business management. Phillip, who himself was an excellent basketball player before, trained his son to be a world famous player. It is his father who pushed O'Neal to the brilliant throne of NBA.

O'Neal succeeds. He is another superstar after Michael Jordan and Magic Johnson of NBA.

Choose the right answer:

(   ) 1. The passage tells us something about O'Neal except _____.
　　A. his appearance 　　　　　B. his parents
　　C. his hard work in NBA 　　D. his personality

(   ) 2. Which of the following is NOT well-known in NBA?
　　A. Phillip. 　　　　　　　　B. Shark O'Neal.
　　C. Michael Jordan. 　　　　D. Magic Johnson.

(   ) 3. "Orando Magics" is the name of _____.
　　A. a famous football coach
　　B. a city which is famous for basketball
　　C. a famous basketball team
　　D. Shark O'Neal's cousin

(   ) 4. In the passage "Black Horse" means _____.
　　A. a black player 　　　　　B. a black NBA player
　　C. a black American 　　　　D. a rising superstar

(   ) 5. Which of the following sentences is NOT true?
　　A. Shark O'Neal is thought to be a billionaire in three years.
　　B. Phillip did a lot for O'Neal's honour today.
　　C. Shark O'Neal gets a lot of money from his fans.
　　D. Shark O'Neal is a black American.

13

Lei Feng was born on December 18th, 1940 in a poor peasant family in Hunan Province. He became a homeless orphan at seven and made a living by cutting firewood for others. The poor life lasted until 1949 when New China was founded. With the help of the local government, he received a primary school education.

In 1960, he joined the PLA. One day, he set off for Liaoning Province on business. When an old woman couldn't find a seat on the crowded train, Lei Feng offered his to her at once. Then he cleaned the car and filled the passengers' bottles with hot water. "You need a break, son." said a grandmother when she saw the sweat(汗) running down his face. "Oh, don't worry. I'm just fine," he replied.

Lei Feng was happy to do things for others. He is famous for his words, "Life is short, but the cause(事业) of serving others is limitless(无限的). I have decided to devote my limited life to serving the people." He kept his words. We should learn from Comrade Lei Feng.

Choose the right answer:

( ) 1. Why did Lei Feng have to make a living by cutting firewood?

    A. Because he had nothing else to do.

    B. Because he liked cutting firewood.

    C. Because he had no parents, and he did that to make money.

    D. Because his parents asked him to do so.

( ) 2. How old was Lei Feng when he joined the PLA?

    A. Over 20.   B. 20.   C. 30.   D. Over 30.

( ) 3. Was Lei Feng always happy to help others?

    A. Yes, he was.   B. No, sometimes.

    C. Yes, only when he was happy.   D. No, not vey often.

( ) 4. What kind of person was Lei Feng?

    A. Great.   B. Kind-hearted.   C. Helpful.   D. A, B and C.

( ) 5. What does the sentence "He kept his words." mean?

    A. He kept his words on his book.

    B. He did everything as he said.

    C. He put his words into his pocket.

    D. He kept every word he said.

14

Bill Gates was born in Seattle in 1955. Young Gates's grades weren't always great. He didn't find his interest until in the eighth grade. In the 1960s, the Mothers' Club at Gates's school bought a computer for the students. Gates learned about it and soon became a computer fan. In fact, he was so crazy about programming that he later left Harvard without finishing his studies. He formed a company with his friend Paul Allen and started his own business.

The early years were hard. Gates often worked late into the night and sometimes slept under his desk. Today, Microsoft is the greatest in software industry. As the chairman of Microsoft, Gates is regarded as the prince of programmers. Those who know him best describe Gates as a diligent and clever man.

Although Gates is very rich, he hasn't slowed down his work. He is still a workaholic(工作狂). In his office, he keeps a picture of Henry Ford. It can tell Gates that he needs to work hard as he wants to lead his company and industry better to the future.

In the year of 2008, as a 53-year-old man, Gates finally retired from his work. Instead of giving his money to his children, Gates decided to donate it to charity. He wants to use his money to help those people with AIDS disease all over the world. What a generous and great man Bill Gates is!

Choose the right answer:

( ) 1. Bill Gates _____.

    A. was crazy about playing games in Grade 8

    B. is good at making computers

    C. was the chairman of Microsoft before the year of 2008

    D. was always the top student in his school

( ) 2. When did Bill Gates become interested in computers?

    A. After he started his own business.

    B. In the 1960s.

    C. After he left Harvard.

    D. In 1955.

( ) 3. Bill Gates formed a company _____.

    A. after he finished Harvard   B. to help his friend Paul Allen

    C. when he was in Grade 8   D. before he finished Harvard

( ) 4. Bill Gates keeps a picture of Henry Ford in his office _____.

    A. to enjoy the beautiful picture

    B. to make people know who is Henry Ford

    C. to tell himself to work hard for a better future

    D. because Henry Ford is his friend

( ) 5. How did Bill Gates use his money after he retired from his work?

    A. To form another computer company.

    B. To give the money to his children.

    C. To travel around the world with his family.

    D. To donate the money to charity and help those people with AIDS disease.

15

Yang Liwei was born in 1965. At 18, he became a college student. He worked hard and trained himself into a good pilot. In 1998, he was chosen to be a spaceman. He knew it was very important to do this work. He worked harder and more carefully than before.

At about 6:15 am on October. 15th, 2003, Yang Liwei stepped into the craft with a smile on his face. At 9:00 am, he was sent into space in China's Shenzhou Ⅴ spacecraft. During his stay in space, he wrote down what happened around him and searched for information people need. At last, he successfully came back to the earth after a 21-hour trip in space.

Chinese people were excited, and they greeted him with lots of flowers. And people all over the world were surprised to see the great endeavour(尝试) of China. China has become the third country in the world to send a manned(载人的) spaceship into space independently(独立地).

Choose the right answer:

(   ) 1. Yang Liwei _____ in the college.
      A. travelled a lot   B. became a spaceman
      C. became a good pilot   D. went to space

(   ) 2. Yang Liwei was sent up into space at the age of _____.
      A. 20   B. 38   C. 25   D. 28

(   ) 3. He seemed _____ when he stepped into the spaceship.
      A. nervous   B. worried   C. surprised   D. happy

(   ) 4. He travelled in space for _____.
      A. 21 hours   B. 21 days   C. 21 minutes   D. 21-hour

(   ) 5. China is the _____ country to send a manned spaceship into space.
      A. first   B. second   C. third   D. fourth

16

Early in the eighteenth century, there was a famous English explorer called Captain Cook. One day he saw an unusual animal during his first visit to Australia. The animal had a large mouse-like head and jumped along on its large legs. To his great surprise, the unusual animal carried its young baby in a special pocket of flesh. Captain Cook pointed to the animal and asked his local guide what the animal was. The guide seemed not to know what he was pointing at and finally said, "Kang-a-roo." Cook carefully wrote down the animal's name in his word book. The Europeans who later got to Australia were looking forward to seeing the unusual animal "kang-a-roo", but their requests were met with puzzled looks of the local people. They soon found that "kang-a-roo" really meant "I don't know what you mean." This is how the word "kangaroo" has come into use.

Choose the right answer:

(   ) 1. Captain Cook was _____.

A. an American scientist　　　　B. an Australian explorer

C. an Englishman　　　　D. a great guide

(　) 2. Captain Cook reached Australia about _____.

A. 300 years ago　　　　B. 100 years ago

C. 400 years ago　　　　D. 50 years ago

(　) 3. A mother kangaroo carries her baby _____.

A. in her arms　　　　B. on the tree

C. on her back　　　　D. in a special pocket of flesh

(　) 4. The word "kang-a-roo" meant _____.

A. I don't know who you are　　　　B. a special animal

C. I don't know what you mean　　　　D. a funny animal

(　) 5. The best title of this passage is _____.

A. A Story of Kangaroo　　　　B. Captain Cook

C. Travel in Australia　　　　D. Captain Cook's Book

17

Walt Disney was born in Chicago in 1901. He enjoyed drawing. He was very poor. He drew pictures in his father's garage. One day a mouse came into the garage and played on the floor. Disney gave him some bread. Then the mouse came up and sat on his desk. In this way, the mouse and the poor artist became good friends.

Later Disney went to Hollywood. He worked very hard, but he was not known to many people.

One day he remembered the mouse. "I will draw that mouse," said to himself. "I hope every child in this country will like my mouse."

He drew many pictures of the mouse. At last he was pleased with one of his pictures. The mouse was called Mickey Mouse. Soon Mickey Mouse was known all over the world. And the name of Walt Disney is known to many people in the world, too. Now Disneyland is the world's greatest park for children.

Choose the right answer：

(　) 1. Walt Disney was born in _____.

A. China　　　B. England　　　C. Canada　　　D. America

(　) 2. The mouse in the garage became his good friend because _____.

A. the mouse was friendly　　　　B. the mouse liked sitting on his desk

C. he gave the mouse bread to eat　　　D. the mouse liked his pictures

(　) 3. Before Mickey Mouse was born, Disney was _____.

A. well known all over the world　　　B. well known in Chicago

C. well know in Hollywood　　　　D. an unknown poor artist

( ) 4. Mickey Mouse was _____.

    A. the name of the mouse in the garage

    B. the name of the mouse drawn by Disney

    C. a lovely mouse in Chicago

    D. born in Chicago in 1901

( ) 5. Walt Disney became known to many people because of _____.

    A. Mickey Mouse   B. Disneyland

    C. his father's garage   D. moving to Hollywood

18

The 26-year-old Sui Feifei shines in basketball games. She is known as "beauty" on the basketball court.

Sui Feifei has been on China's women basketball team for many years, but now she has a new life: playing in the WNBA(美国女子职业篮球联赛) for Sacramento Monarchs (萨克拉门托君主队) in the USA. It's the first time for Sui to work and live abroad. She says she is ready for the challenge ahead. She shows great <u>confidence</u>, and this comes mostly from her good spoken English.

When she went to get her visa, she talked happily with the officer there, and even gave the officer a lesson in basketball in English. "My best point is that I enjoy speaking—I'm never afraid to open my mouth!" she says. She likes speaking to any foreigner.

Off the court, Sui is a good writer. Her love of writing comes from having read widely, even Kung Fu stories. Sui writes for many newspapers, but she also enjoys keeping diaries. She feels free to put her thoughts down on a piece of paper. Sui looks nice but she doesn't want to be liked just for her beauty. "As for me, the courage and wisdom on court shows the real beauty, not a pretty face." she says.

Choose the right answer:

( ) 1. Sui Feifei is one of the best basketball players in _____.

    A. England   B. China

    C. Sacramento Monarchs   D. the USA

( ) 2. Many people know Sui Feifei because she _____.

    A. is not only good at basketball but also beautiful

    B. is the only Chinese girl playing in the WNBA in the USA

    C. is the most beautiful girl in China

    D. is the best basketball player in the world

( ) 3. The underlined word "confidence" means "_____" in Chinese.

    A. 智慧   B. 勇气   C. 自信   D. 决心

（　　）4. Sui can speak English quite well because she ＿＿＿＿.

    A.　often goes abroad　　　　　B.　learned it hard at school

    C.　practises it very often　　　　D.　is an American

（　　）5. Which of the following is true?

    A.　Sui wants people to notice her pretty face on the basketball court.

    B.　In her spare time, Sui enjoys reading and writing.

    C.　When she is free, Sui doesn't like to write down what she thinks.

    D.　She is proud of her pretty face.

19

An Wang was born in Shanghai, China, in 1920. He came to America as an immigrant at the age of twenty-five. He studied at Harvard, a famous university near Boston. He was very intelligent and soon got a decorate from Harvard.

In 1951 An Wang started a small company. The company was Wang Laboratories. It had only one room and two employees. The company made calculators and computers. Each year the company grew and grew. By 1985 Wang had thirty thousand employees and had made $3 billion. Wang was one of the most successful computer companies in the world.

Money didn't change An Wang. He lived with his wife in the same house outside Boston. He had only two suits at one time, and they were very gray. An Wang's life was his company. He made his son, Fred, president of the company in 1986. The company began to have problems.

Wang died in 1990. People in America will remember this great man. He was generous and liked to give money. We find his name in places like the Wang Center for the Performing Arts or the Wang Institute in Boston.

Choose the right answer：

（　　）1. The main character An Wang in the passage came from ＿＿＿＿.

    A.　China　　　　B.　Harvard　　　　C.　Boston　　　　D.　America

（　　）2. In 1951 Wang Laboratories ＿＿＿＿.

    A.　was the most successful company in the world

    B.　was a small company

    C.　had 30 000 employees

    D.　had made $3 billion

（　　）3. Wang's life was his ＿＿＿＿.

    A.　money　　　　B.　house　　　　C.　company　　　　D.　family

（　　）4. People in America will never forget An Wang because ＿＿＿＿.

A. he was an immigrant

B. he had made ＄3 billion

C. he was kind and noble-minded(品德高尚的)

D. he built the Wang Institute in Boston

(　　) 5. When did he die? He died when he was _____.

A. in his seventieth 　　　　B. at the age of seventy

C. more than seventy 　　　　D. less than seventy

20

Stephen Hawking was born in Oxford，England on 8th January，1942. He went to school in St Alban—a small city near London. Although he did well，he was never top of his class. After leaving school，Hawking went first to Oxford University where he studied physics，then he went to Cambridge University where he studied cosmology. As he himself admitted(承认)，he didn't work hard. He was a very lazy student，and did very little work. However，he still got good marks.

It was at the age of 20 that Hawking first noticed something was wrong with him. He started to bump(撞上) into something. When he visited his family at Christmas time，his mother was so worried that she made him see a doctor. Hawking was sent to hospital for tests. Finally，the result came back. Hawking had motor neurone disease，an incurable illness which would make him unable to speak，breathe or move without the help of a machine. Doctors said they had no way to help him. He would die before he was 23.

At first，Hawking became very depressed (忧伤的). After a while，though，he began to see his life in a different way. As he later wrote，"Before my illness was diagnosed(诊断)，I had been very bored with life. There had not seemed to be anything worth doing. But shortly after I came out of hospital，I suddenly realized that there were a lot of worthwhile things I could do." Hawking married，found a job at Cambridge University，and had three children. He also went on to do some of the most important scientific research.

Today，Hawking still works at Cambridge University as a professor. He strongly believes that his story shows that nobody，however bad their situation(处境) is，should lose hope. "Life is not fair，" he once said，"you just have to do the best you can in your own situation."

Choose the right answer：

(　　) 1. As a university student，Stephen Hawking _____.

A. worked very hard 　　　　B. studied maths and physics

C. was the best student in his class D. was lazy and did very little work

（　　）2. Hawking first noticed something was wrong with him when _____.

A. he was sent to hospital for tests

B. his mother made him see a doctor

C. he was twenty

D. he visited his family at Christmas time one year

（　　）3. In this passage the underlined word "incurable" means "_____".

A. 无法治愈的　　　　　　B. 难以确诊的

C. 常见的　　　　　　　　D. 可以治愈的

（　　）4. When Hawking was first diagnosed with motor neurone disease，he _____.

A. made up his mind to get married

B. began to see his life in a different way

C. became very sad

D. thought that nothing in life was worth doing

（　　）5. What would be the best title（题目）for this passage?

A. Motor Neurone Disease.　　　B. Life Is Fair.

C. Professor Stephen Hawking.　　D. A Lazy Boy.

 体育类

🖊 范文解析

Almost everybody likes to play. All over the world men and women，boys and girls enjoy sports. Sports help to keep people healthy. They help people to live happily.

Sports change with the season. People play different games in winter and summer. Sailing is fun in warm weather，while skating is good in winter.

Games and sports often grow out of the work people do. The Arabs are famous for their horses and camels. They use them in their work，and they use them in their sports events，too. Hunting and fishing are very good sports. But millions of people hunt and fish for a living.

People from different countries may not be able to understand each other，but after a game on the sports field，they often become good friends. Sports help to train a person's character. One learns to fight fair and hard，to win without pride and to lose with grace.

True or False：

（　　）1. Almost everyone enjoys sports.

（　　）2. Sports can help people to keep healthy and to live happily.

(　　) 3. People have different sports in different seasons.

(　　) 4. The Arabs only like horses and camels.

(　　) 5. People from different countries can't understand each other or be good friends.

【答案与解析】

1. **T**　可从文中前两句"Almost everybody likes to play. All over the world men and women，boys and girls enjoy sports."得知世界上几乎每个人都喜欢体育运动。

2. **T**　可由文章第一段最后两句"Sports help to keep people healthy. They help people to live happily."直接得知。

3. **T**　可由文章第二段前两句"Sports change with the season. People play different games in winter and summer."得知人们所进行的体育运动是随季节的变化而变化的。

4. **F**　文章第3段中提到"The Arabs are famous for their horses and camels. They use them in their work，and they use them in their sports events，too."这告诉我们，阿拉伯人因他们的马和骆驼而闻名于世。他们将马与骆驼用在劳动和体育运动中。由此我们只能得知，阿拉伯人肯定很喜欢马与骆驼这两种动物，但不能表示他们不喜欢其他的动物。因此我们不能直接说"The Arabs only like horses and camels."

5. **F**　仔细阅读文章最后一段中的这句话"People from different countries may not be able to understand each other，but after a game on the sports field，they often become good friends."由此我们知道，不同国家的人们起初虽不能互相理解，但往往在一起进行过一次体育比赛后，他们就会互相成为朋友。而第5题的句子是绝对的否定句，意思是不同国家的人们不可能互相理解，也不可能成为好朋友。这显然与原文意思不符合。

实战演练

1

The word "sport" first meant something that people did in their free time. Later it often meant hunting wild animals and birds.

About a hundred years ago the word was first used for organized games. This is the usual meaning of the word today. People spend a lot of their spare time playing football, basketball, tennis and many other sports. Such people play because they want to. A few people are paid for the sport they play. These people are called professional sportsmen. They may be sportsmen for only a few years, but during that time the best one can earn a lot of money.

For example, a professional footballer in England earns more than $3 000 a year. The stars earn a lot more. International golf and tennis champions can make more than $50 000 in a year. Of course, only a few sportsmen can earn as much money as that. It is only possible in sports for individuals like golf, tennis and motor-racing. Perhaps the most surprising thing about sportsmen and money is this: The stars can earn more money from advertising than from sport. An advertising for sports equipment(运动装备) does not simply say "Buy our thing". It says " Buy the same shirt and shoes as…". Famous sportsmen can even advertise things like watches and food. They allow the companies to use their names or photographs and they are paid for this. Sport is no longer just something for people's spare time.

Choose the right answer:

( ) 1. A "professional" sportsman is someone who _____.

A. earns a lot of money B. plays a sport for a number of years

C. likes sport very much D. earns money by playing a sport

( ) 2. The word "sport" now usually means _____.

A. professional games

B. hunting wild animals and birds

C. games played during people's spare time

D. organized games

( ) 3. An advertisement for sports equipment _____ "Buy our things".

A. do not simply say B. does not simply say

C. simply says not D. simply does not say

( ) 4. "Spare time" means _____ time.

A. own B. happy C. free D. home

( ) 5. Which is the best topic of this passage?

A. People's Spare Time. B. Sportsmen and Advertisement.

C. Sport and Money. D. Professional Sportsmen.

2

Until 1871, everyone in England played football for fun. Then someone had the idea of giving a beautiful cup to the best team each year. The Football Association agreed. It made rules for its teams.

Today in the FA Cup, teams play against each other until there is only one team left, the winning team. The winners get the Cup. Any team, large or small, important or unimportant, in or out the association, can play, but it is very hard to get the Cup.

The FA Cup is often just called "the Cup". There are other cups(like the League Cup(联合杯), for example), but "the Cup" always means the "big one". To win it is as good as winning the League, perhaps even better. At the end of the game, one team is the best of all. The players stand there in front of many people, sometimes more than fifty thousand, and one by one, each of the eleven members of the team holds the great

Cup above his head. It is one of the greatest moments of England football.

Choose the right answer：

( ) 1. In the early days people played football for _____ .
  A. an idea   B. fun
  C. drinking cups   D. the Cup

( ) 2. In the FA Cup，there is one team left at last. It is the _____ one.
  A. best   B. largest   C. important   D. last

( ) 3. When people talk about "the Cup"，we know that they are talking about _____ .
  A. FA Cup   B. League Cup
  C. better one   D. other cup

( ) 4. There are always _____ the final game.
  A. many people watching   B. two teams holding the cup in
  C. fifty thousand people playing   D. only eleven players playing

( ) 5. From the passage we can see that _____ .
  A. it is also hard to get the League Cup
  B. it is not easy to take part in the FA Cup game
  C. each team of the FA has a cup every year
  D. each member of the winning team gets a cup

3

The Olympic Games are held every four years in a different city in the world. Athletes from many countries compete(竞赛) in a variety of sports. These sports are divided into winter and summer games.

The Olympics began in Greece more than 2 700 years ago. The games were originally part of a religious festival(宗教节日) in honour of the Greek God. Eventually，the games became the most important festival in all of Greece.

The first recorded Olympic competition was held in 776BC. It was held in an outdoor stadium which was about 200 metres long and 30 metres wide. The stadium was in a valley，and about forty thousand people watched the event. The first thirteen Olympics had only one race—running.

Since 776BC，the games had been held regularly for about 1 200 years. In 397 the Olympics were prohibited(禁止) by the Roman Emperor(罗马教皇).

It was not until 1896 when the first Olympics of modern times were held in Athens (雅典). From then on，the games are held every four years regularly. The Olympics have become the world's most important athletic events and a symbol(标志) of the sporting friendship of all the people of the world.

Choose the right answer：

(　　) 1. The 26th Olympic Games was held in America in 1996 and the next one was held in Sydney in _____.

      A. 1994　　　　　B. 1996　　　　　C. 2000　　　　　D. 1998

(　　) 2. _____ Olympics there was only one race-running.

      A. Only the first and the thirteenth

      B. Only the thirteenth

      C. From the first to the thirteenth

      D. At thirteen

(　　) 3. The Olympics were prohibited for _____.

      A. more than 14 centuries　　　　　B. more than 16 centuries

      C. more than 20 centuries　　　　　D. less than 13 centuries

(　　) 4. Which of the following is discussed in the passage?

      A. The Greek God.

      B. The history of the Olympic Games.

      C. The place and the time of every Olympic Games.

      D. The Roman Emperor.

(　　) 5. Why do the Olympic Games seem so important to the people all over the world?

      A. They are the most important sporting events.

      B. They promote(提倡) friendship among the people all over the world and make great contributions(贡献) to the world peace.

      C. They are held in different places of the world.

      D. They tell the people all over the world what sports are.

4

Running is an easy activity to do and enjoy. You can run almost anywhere and you only need shoes. Running is good for your whole body and mind. It is a great time to just think or even talk with a friend, a coach, or a parent. You can run short distances, middle distances, and build up to long distances. It is important to find a way to keep on running. Enter a school, or enter a few races and run with your friends and parents. Sometimes all you need is a running buddy and time.

Running can be fun if you feel well and you will enjoy doing it. You can also try our races or triathlons(swim, bike, run) for fun. But remember that too much exercise is unhealthy and it can make you feel tired and hurt you, so run just until you are comfortable. If you are training for an event, a coach can help you build up to the distance and teach you how to pace(协调) yourself for that race. Running is a great way to have fun and keep fit，but it is also important to remember to run safely and enjoy it.

True or False：

（　　）1. Running is very easy because you can run almost anywhere and you only need shoes.

（　　）2. You have to run alone every time because it is better for your body and mind.

（　　）3. Running can always be fun.

（　　）4. Instead of running too much，you should run until you are comfortable.

（　　）5. Running is a great way to have fun and keep fit.

5

The baseball season goes from April to September. During this time，people can watch baseball matches on TV and members of the important baseball teams become American heroes. At the end of the season the two top teams will play against each other. Many baseball fans go along to watch the game. Millions of others listen to the radio and watch TV. People seem to talk only about the game. Even long after it is over，they still talk about the result and the players.

American football is the most popular sport in the USA. The football season begins when the baseball season ends. More people like football better than baseball. When there is an important game，thousands of people will sit beside the radio or in front of the TV set to wait for the result.

True or False：

（　　）1. The baseball season lasts for four months.

（　　）2. During the baseball season members of the important baseball teams become American heroes.

（　　）3. American people stop talking about the result and players as soon as the baseball season is over.

（　　）4. American football is the most popular sport in the USA.

（　　）5. Baseball is less popular than American football in the USA.

6

Swimming is very popular in summer. People like swimming in summer because water makes people feel cool. If you like swimming but swim in a wrong place，it may not be safe. These years，more than ten people died while they were enjoying themselves in the water，and most of them were students. But some people are still not careful in swimming. They often think they swim so well that nothing will happen to them in water. Summer is here again. If you go swimming in summer，don't forget that better swimmers have died in water. They died because they were not careful, not because they could not swim. So don't get into water when you are alone. If there is a "No swimming" sign, don't get into the water, either. If you remember these, swimming will be safe.

True or False:

(　　) 1. A lot of people like swimming in summer because water can make them cool.

(　　) 2. Swimming in a wrong place can be dangerous.

(　　) 3. After many students died while they were enjoying themselves in the water, all the people become careful in swimming.

(　　) 4. If you are a good swimmer, then don't worry about the possibility of death when you are swimming anywhere.

(　　) 5. Don't get into water if you are alone or there is a "No swimming" sign.

Diving is a new sport today. This sport takes you into a wonderful new world. It is like a visit to the moon! When you are under water, it is easy for you to climb big rocks, because you are no longer heavy.

Here under water, everything is blue and green. During the day, there is enough light under water. When fish swim nearby, you can catch them with your hands.

When you have tanks of air on your back, you can stay in deep water for a long time. But you must be careful when you dive in deep water.

To catch fish is one of the most interesting parts of this sport. Besides, there are more uses for diving. You can clean ships without taking them out of the water. You can get many things from the deep sea.

Now you can see that diving is both useful and interesting.

True or False:

(　　) 1. Diving is a new sport which can take you into a wonderful new world.

(　　) 2. When you are under water, you can easily climb big rocks because you are near them.

(　　) 3. When you have tanks of air on your back, you can stay in deep water for a long time.

(　　) 4. To catch fish is the most interesting part of diving.

(　　) 5. Diving is not only interesting, but also useful.

8

Push-ups are a new kind of exercise that you can do to make your body strong. In order to do a push-up correctly, first lie down on the floor, face down. Keep your legs together. As you lie on the floor, put your hands on the floor next to your shoulders.

Now push your body away from the floor. Straighten your arms so that you can push your body up. Your body is held by your arms and toes. Your body should be a straight line. Next, lower your body again slowly. Stop when your chest almost touches the floor. In other words, when your chest is very next to the floor, stop lowering yourself. Push yourself again at once. When you lower yourself and push yourself up once, you have done one push-up.

In middle schools boys like doing push-ups very much. And they are asked to do push-ups in their PE lessons by their teachers. Many boys are able to do at least ten push-ups at a time. But it's not easy for some weak boys to do push-ups. Maybe they haven't got right ways to do them. What about you?

True or False:

( ) 1. Push-ups are a new kind of exercise that you can do to make your body thin and slim.

( ) 2. You should lie down on the floor and keep your face down if you want to do a push-up.

( ) 3. When you do a push-up, your body is held by your hands and back.

( ) 4. When you do a push-up, you should stop lowering yourself when your chest is close to the floor.

( ) 5. All the school boys can do push-ups very easily.

9

It was time for the first race. The race-horses were ready to start.

Whish(飕飕声), whoosh(嘶嘶声)! Away ran Dobbo to join them.

The race-horses were just starting. Farmer Smith shouted. All the people shouted. Some people laughed. Bill the Bull looked over the fence and laughed. Dobbo took no notice. He was a race-horse now.

The race-horses ran like the wind. How fast they ran! Poor Dobbo was left far behind. He could not catch them. He ran as fast as he could, but he could not catch them.

His heart went thump, thump, thump(怦怦地跳). He was out of breath. His legs ached. Oh, how tired he was!

At last he came to a stop, a long way behind the other horses. He could hear people laughing at him.

"Just look at that cart-horse(拖货车的马)," they said. "He thinks he is a race-horse. How foolish he is!"

Then Dobbo knew he would never be a race-horse. He was too big and heavy. He was only a cart-horse. He would never be really important.

Choose the right answer:

( ) 1. What was the farmer's name?

    A. Bull.   B. Jones.   C. Smith.   D. Bill.

( ) 2. Why did Dobbo run after the race-horses? Because _____.

    A. he felt happy and cheerful

    B. his master told him to run

    C. he wanted to be a race-horse

    D. he was pushed out by other horses

( ) 3. Which kind of horse was Dobbo?

    A. A race-horse.   B. A cart-horse.

    C. A foolish horse.   D. A clever horse.

( ) 4. Why couldn't Dobbo run as fast as the race-horse? Because _____.

    A. he was too big   B. he was too heavy

    C. he was only a race-horse   D. both A and B

( ) 5. What does the underlined phrase "took no notice" mean?

    A. didn't take any notice.   B. didn't pay attention to.

    C. didn't take any notes.   D. didn't see any notice.

10

You may have known quite a lot about the modern Olympic Games, especially the Summer Games, which began in Greece in 1896. But how much do you know about special games for the disabled?

The first Special Olympic Games was held in Rome in 1960. Now soon after every Summer Games, the host city holds a Special Olympic Games, such as the games in Barcelona in 1992 and in Atlanta in 1996. Over the years, it has grown into one of the largest sporting events for the disabled in the world. Many people who watched the games said that they were greatly impressed by the effort and courage shown through the games.

All the sportsmen who took part in the special games had a common goal: they wanted to prove to themselves and to the world that they were full of life and hope, and that they were willing to try and eager to learn.

The games also offer the rest of the world a chance to learn more about the disabled by watching them competing against each other. Their beliefs, their dreams and their efforts are all on show for the world to see. People watching the games realize that "special" people are really no different in their aims from others.

Choose the right answer:

( ) 1. The Special Olympic Games began _____.

      A. in Greece in 1896   B. in Rome in 1960

      C. in Barcelon in 1992   D. in Atlanta in 1996

(   ) 2. The Special Olympic Games are held _____.

      A. before long after the Summer Olympic Games

      B. in a short time after the Winter Olympic Games

      C. before the Summer Olympic Games

      D. between the Summer Olympic Games and the Winter Olympic Games

(   ) 3. From 1990 to 2000, how many special games might be held?

      A. Ten.   B. Five.   C. Three.   D. One.

(   ) 4. Who will NOT take part in the special games?

      A. The blind people.   B. The deaf people.

      C. The arm-lost people.   D. The sick people.

(   ) 5. Which of the following is TRUE according to the passage?

      A. The disabled dislike the special games, because they aren't willing to learn and try.

      B. The disabled want to get more sympathy(同情) by the games.

      C. The disabled like Summer Games better than the special games.

      D. The disabled are willing to try and eager to learn and they want to show their dreams and beliefs through the special games.

11

Last month, Sam Lee from Hong Kong took part in a high school adventure trip to Mount Huangshan, one of the most famous mountains in China. It is well-known for its beautiful scenery. "I have known about the mountain since I saw the film *Crouching Tiger, Hidden Dragon*. I felt that it must be a wonderful place to visit, so when I had the chance to go, I signed up. We don't have any mountains as high as Mount Huangshan in Hong Kong. I knew it would be an unforgettable experience." "Members in our group woke up early every morning and began climbing. Trying to get up early every morning was really not easy for me." Sam said with a laugh. Sam remembered one of the most difficult climbs when they were climbing up to the Lotus Peak, the highest point of Mount Huangshan. They hiked all day, with only short breaks in-between. But finally Sam saw the most beautiful view he had never seen before. Then, what was the best part of the trip for Sam? "I learnt that I could do anything I wanted to do as long as I put my mind to it. There were times when I thought I couldn't make it to the top because I was so tired. But then I just kept encouraging myself. Keeping a good mood is important, especially when things get tough."

Choose the right answer:

(   ) 1. Mount Huangshan is famous for _____.

       A. the beautiful view

       B. its height

       C. *Crouching Tiger，Hidden Dragon*

       D. the Lotus Peak

(   ) 2. Sam wanted to go to Mount Huangshan because _____.

       A. his friends invited him

       B. he saw a film about the mountain and it looked really beautiful in the film

       C. he read a book about it

       D. he heard a lot about it

(   ) 3. Sam kept cheering himself up when _____.

       A. climbing the mountain   B. getting up early every morning

       C. things were getting better   D. he was in a good mood

(   ) 4. What's the meaning of the underlined word "in-between"?

       A. 两者之一   B. 在两次   C. 在中间   D. 在两座山里面

(   ) 5. The best part of the trip was _____.

       A. realizing that anything is possible if you put your mind to it

       B. seeing the view from the top of the mountain

       C. seeing the sunrise every morning

       D. when Sam saw the film during the trip

12

Not long ago the famous British tournament at the All England Lawn Tennis Club opened. Almost 500 000 fans were attracted and players from 60 nations came for competing. Across the world 1.8 billion people were following the action on the television，radio and Internet.

It's the oldest tennis tournament in the world. The first Wimbledon championships (锦标赛) was held by a private club as a relaxing party in 1877. Just 22 players took part，and no more than a few hundred spectators came to watch. But these days the Lawn Tennis Championship at Wimbledon is the third Grand Slam tournament played each year. It's after the Australian Open and the French Open，and followed by the US Open.

Wimbledon is widely known for its special rules and traditions. The players' clothing，including their shoes，must be entirely white. The United Kingdom's changeable summer weather is part of the tournament. If rain begins to fall，the players and fans have to wait patiently for it to stop. Then，they cheer as the covers come off the grass court.

Wimbledon is not just famous for great tennis matches. Fans like to eat strawberries and cream while watching. Every year 27 000 kilos of strawberries are eaten up and 7 000 litres of cream.

True or False：

(　) 1. According to the passage above, tennis is one of the most popular sports around the world.

(　) 2. The Wimbledon Championships is the world's biggest tennis tournament.

(　) 3. One tradition of the game is that players are required to wear all white on court.

(　) 4. In Wimbledon championships, if rain begins to fall, the players and fans have to wait patiently for it to stop.

(　) 5. People will eat a lot of strawberries and ice cream while watching the matches.

13

Last week all classes in Beijing Sunshine Secondary School decided who had the best moves at an exciting group dance competition.

Shi Shi, aged 16, and her classmates performed the Latin cha-cha. They chose this dance because they thought few classes would try such a passionate style. Rounds of applause showed their hours of practice paid off. "We invited two junior school girls who attend a dancing school to teach us basic movements. Then we practised to the music at lunchtime and after school and for many hours at the weekend," Shi said.

To create an impressive scene, students carefully prepared their clothes. Class 12, Senior 3 rented Tibetan clothes from a store to perform a Tibetan dance. "All my classmates tried their best because it was the last chance for us to do an activity together before finishing our time of high school," an 18-year-old girl said.

Doing the right moves was important, Luo Yu thinks. Her class took first place with the dance of *Goddess With a Thousand Arms*. The dance group found out a video on the Internet of the dance as it was shown on 2005 Spring Festival Gala. "We watched the video many times and believed that our dance could be as wonderful as the one performed by the disabled artists." Luo said.

Even though they were busy with their studies, the students had great fun and found a new way to relax.

Choose the right answer：

(　) 1. Why did Shi and her classmates perform the Latin cha-cha?

　　　　A. Because all of them liked the passionate style.

B. Because few classes chose to dance it.

C. Because they had learned it from two junior school girls.

D. Because it was easy to learn.

( ) 2. When did the student dancers practise their dancing?

A. In their free time.　　　　 B. On Sunday.

C. In suppertime.　　　　　 D. On weekdays.

( ) 3. What did Class 12 rent Tibetan clothes from a clothing store for?

A. A modern dance.　　　　 B. A folk dance.

C. A ballet.　　　　　　　 D. A ballroom dance.

( ) 4. How did Luo Yu learn to dance *Goddess With a Thousand Arms*?

A. She learned it from a CCTV programme.

B. She learned it from a group of disabled people.

C. She learned it from a video on the Internet.

D. She learned it from her class monitor.

( ) 5. What did the students think of the dance competition?

A. Relaxing.　　 B. Boring.　　 C. Funny.　　 D. Busy.

14

Basketball is an American game. A man named James Nailsmith made it up in 1891. He wanted a game to play inside in the winter. The first real game was played in 1892.

Nailsmith put up two peach baskets. There were nine players on each side. The players tried to throw the ball into the baskets. There were no holes in the bottom of the baskets. When a ball went into the basket, it stayed there. The game had to stop. A player climbed up to get the ball. It was a slow game. After a while, people used net baskets. They cut the bottoms out of the baskets.

At first, many persons could play. Now only ten team members play the game. There are five players on each side. Basketball today is a very fast game.

Choose the right answer:

( ) 1. "_____" in the passage means "a sport".

A. Bottom　　 B. Game　　 C. Player　　 D. Basket

( ) 2. How many team members played the game at first?

A. Ten.　　　　　　　　　 B. Five.

C. Nine.　　　　　　　　　 D. Eighteen.

( ) 3. What happened when the ball went into the peach basket?

A. It stayed there.

B. The players must cut out the bottom.

C. It dropped through the basket.

D. The players had to call Nailsmith.

(　　) 4. From the passage we know that _____.

A. all the games are not much interesting

B. basketball began as a farmers' game

C. Nailsmith invented basketball in 1891

D. we still use peach baskets when we play this game today

(　　) 5. The best title for this passage is _____.

A. Fast Game 　　　　　　B. The Sport of Basketball

C. The Best Game In the World 　　D. Something About James Nailsmith

15

Football is one of the most popular, interesting and exciting games. Football is popular among tens of millions of people all over the world.

I am a football fan. I began to watch football games when the League Football Match first took place in China. Then, I became interested in football. In the match, I enjoy the wonderful goal shootings and the players' courage and endurance. The most interesting thing is the result which anyone can hardly tell.

The World Cup is held every four years. It draws a lot of interest of people all over the world when teams from different countries begin to fight for the World Cup. In the match, many football fans make friends with one another and know different things of other countries. So football match is not a simple match. It's an exchange of culture.

It is good to support your favourite football team on the sport. To support our national team to fight for the World Cup is the hope of all the Chinese football fans.

Choose the right answer:

(　　) 1. The writer became interested in the football when the League Match was first held _____.

A. in the United States 　　　B. in Brazil

C. in China 　　　　　　D. in a place not mentioned

(　　) 2. According to the passage, football is interesting and exciting because of _____.

A. the wonderful goal shootings

B. an unexpected result

C. the players' courage and endurance

D. all the above

(　　) 3. The World Cup is held _____.

A. every four years 　　　　B. every year

        C. every three years   D. every six years

(   ) 4. What is the writer's point of view about the football match?

        A. A simple match.

        B. An exchange of culture.

        C. A match fighting for the World Cup.

        D. I've no idea.

(   ) 5. As an ordinary spectator(观众), what can you do during the match of the World Cup?

        A. To join the football match as a player.

        B. To support your national team to fight for the World Cup.

        C. To go to the place of the match and watch it.

        D. To become a referee(裁判).

16

Teamwork wins the day

    Twenty-two wins in a row(连续). That is a great record(记录). The NBA hasn't seen that during 40 years. But the Rockets did just that!

    The Rockets won the last 10 games without Yao Ming. They did it with a lot of teamwork.

    Teamwork means everyone plays their part. The head coach(主教练), the superstars and the rest of the team all work hard.

    The Rockets didn't keep winning. They lost to Boston Celtics(波士顿凯尔特人) last Wednesday. But now they are in the NBA history books. And they will go on fighting.

Choose the right answer:

(   ) 1. How long hasn't NBA seen twenty-two wins in a row?

        A. For 10 years.   B. For 20 years.

        C. For 30 years.   D. For 40 years.

(   ) 2. Why could the Rockets win the last 10 games?

        A. Because Yao Ming did lots of good work.

        B. Because their opponents(对手) were all very weak.

        C. Because they did it with a lot of teamwork.

        D. Because they had many fans to support them.

(   ) 3. What does teamwork mean?

        A. It means the head coach and the superstars work hard.

        B. It means the superstars and the rest of the team work hard.

C. It means everyone plays their part and works hard.

D. It means one team works well with another team.

( ) 4. Why didn't the Rockets keep winning?

A. Because Yao Ming didn't take part in the match.

B. Because the whole team became too proud to work hard.

C. Because many players hurt themselves.

D. We don't know from the passage.

( ) 5. Why can the Rockets be in the NBA history books?

A. Because they lost to Boston Celtics.

B. Because they had many superstars in their team.

C. Because they are famous for their teamwork.

D. Because they have twenty-two wins in a row and that is a great record in the NBA history.

17

Bravo! Kobe!

Kobe Bryant has a good reason to be happy this Christmas. He got an early present last week. He became the youngest player to score 20 000 points in the NBA.

It was the end of a great year for the 29-year-old superstar. At the beginning of 2007, his team, the Los Angeles Lakers(洛杉矶湖人队), were not playing well. People said that Bryant would be traded for another player.

But later he was leading the Lakers on a winning streak. He says his future is with the team. He's confident now he's got the record: "It's special to do it," he said of breaking it.

Bryant grew up in Philadelphia(费城). He was lucky because his father Joe was a basketball player. Bryant practiced with one of his father's former teams, the 76ers(费城 76 人队), at the age of 13.

Although he was doing well at school, Bryant didn't go to college. Instead, he joined the Charlotte Hornets(夏洛特黄蜂队). At the age of 18, he became the youngest-ever player to be in an NBA game.

Bryant is cool, quiet and gifted. Many people compare him to Michael Jordan—the NBA's greatest-ever player.

"If there's a player in the NBA who has a chance to be Michael Jordan, I believe this is him. He combines talent with working really hard," says the USA reporter, Neil Curtis.

Choose the right answer:

(   ) 1. Why does Kobe Bryant have a good reason to be happy this Christmas?

    A. Because he got a good present from his family.

    B. Because he became the youngest player to score 20 000 points in the NBA.

    C. Because he would be transferred(转移;转会) into a new team.

    D. Because he was the only player who scored points in his team.

(   ) 2. How did the Los Angeles Lakers play during the year 2007?

    A. At the beginning of 2007 they were not playing well.

    B. Later Kobe Bryant was leading the Lakers on a winning streak.

    C. They played very well during the whole year.

    D. Both A and B.

(   ) 3. What is Kobe's father?

    A. A basketball fan.   B. A basketball coach.

    C. A basketball player.   D. A basketball superstar.

(   ) 4. What did Kobe do at the age of 18?

    A. He went to college and did very well in his study.

    B. He practiced with one of his father's former teams, the 76ers.

    C. He traveled around the country.

    D. He joined the Charlotte Hornets and became the youngest player in an NBA game.

(   ) 5. What do people think of Kobe Bryant?

    A. He is cool, quiet and gifted.

    B. He combines his talent with working really hard.

    C. He has a chance to be Michael Jordan.

    D. All the above.

18

40% people to practice sports regularly in 2010

Xu Chuan, vice-director of the State General Administration of Sports(GAS) mass sports office hopes to see 40 percent of the population exercising regularly(规则地) by 2010. " 'Regular basis' means you exercise at least three times a week at a medium-intense level(中等强度水平), and each time you exercise, it should be at least half an hour," he said in a news conference(新闻发布会)yesterday.

Xu said the ultimate(最终的) goal(目标) of sports is to enhance(增强) people's health. Along with preparation in professional(职业的) and competitive(竞技的) games for the 2008 Olympics, GAS has also launched(进行) a physical fitness campaign(运动)

for the masses consisting of(包含) 65 special events including climbing and dragon boat racing this year.

In a survey(调查) conducted in 2000，34 percent of people exercised regularly. Xu said another survey is currently being conducted, and he expects the number to grow to around 37 percent.

Xu also noted there is still a gap(差距) between China and developed countries in terms of(关于)the number of people exercising regularly due to(由……引起) economic limitations(经济局限).

However，he is not worried about people's passion(热情) for participating in(参与) the special events organized by the government(政府). "A few years ago，we were worried about the turnout(参加人数) of the programs we organized. Now we are concerned about(关注) how to limit(限制) the number of people taking part in these programs," he said.

Choose the right answer：

( ) 1. What does the underlined phrase "regular basis" mean in the passage?

    A. It means you should exercise every day.

    B. It means you should exercise for at least eight hours every week.

    C. It means you should exercise at least three times a week at a medium-intense level，and each time you should exercise at least an hour.

    D. It means you should exercise at least three times a week at a medium-intense level，and each time you should exercise at least half an hour.

( ) 2. What is the ultimate goal of sports according to Xu Chuan?

    A. To make more people take part in the Olympic Games.

    B. To make more people become professional sportsmen.

    C. To make people become healthier and healthier.

    D. To make all the people interested only in sports.

( ) 3. How many people exercised regularly in the survey conducted in 2000?

    A. 34％.   B. 37％.   C. 40％.   D. 65％.

( ) 4. Why are there fewer people exercising regularly in China than in developed countries according to Xu's explanation(解释)?

    A. Because the population in China is smaller than that in developed countries.

    B. Because the population in developed countries is larger than that in China.

    C. Because the economic development(经济发展) in China is not as good as that in developed countries.

    D. Because the economic development in China is as good as that in developed countries.

(   ) 5. According to Xu, what are they concerned about NOW in terms of participating in the special events programs organized by the government?

A. They are concerned about the turnout of the programs.

B. They are concerned about how to make fewer people take part in the programs.

C. They are concerned about how to make more people take part in the programs.

D. They are concerned about people's passion for taking part in the programs.

19

Nadal can still do it!

In some ways Rafael Nadal(纳达尔,西班牙网球新星) is very unlucky. True，the Spaniard(西班牙人) is the world's No. 2 tennis player. He has won the French Open(法国网球公开赛) three times. He has also earned over $15 million. Yet world No. 1 Roger Federer(费得勒,瑞士网球天王), has overshadowed(使……失色) his career(职业生涯).

In the Kingdom(王国) of Tennis, Federer lives in a palace with grass and a big car park. Nadal lives in a smaller house built of clay(红土). Both men prefer to(更喜欢) stay at home rather than play on the other man's ground. Nadal，the King of Clay, has lost to Federer on grass in two Wimbledon finals(温布尔登网球锦标赛决赛). Federer has lost to Nadal on clay in two French Open finals. When they play in Federer's car park on concrete(硬地), like the USA and Australian Opens(美国网球公开赛,澳大利亚网球公开赛), the Swiss(瑞士的) man usually wins. He has seven Grand Slams(大满贯)on hard courts, while Nadal has none.

However, Nadal has won 98 out of his last 99 matches on clay. His most recent(近期的) win came on April 20. He again beat(击败) Federer on clay in the Monte Carlo Masters(蒙特卡罗大师赛). His loss to Federer in 2007 is the only flaw(瑕疵) in his clay court record.

Nadal won his first professional(职业的) tennis match when he was just 15. He seems to have been around for ages, but is still only 22 while Federer is 27. Nadal is a superb(极好的,一流的) athlete(运动员). He has the qualities needed by a truly great tennis player.

Will Nadal be a challenge(挑战) to Federer? Whatever happens, tennis fans should be thankful.

Note：

Grand Slam：大满贯。在网球界,这是网球运动的王冠称号。是指一位或一对网球运动员在同一赛季同时获得温布尔登网球锦标赛、美国网球公开赛、澳大利亚网球公开赛、法国网球公开赛这四大锦标赛的冠军,即为获得大满贯。

Choose the right answer：

( ) 1. What's the difference between Rafael Nadal and Roger Federer?

    A. Nadal is from Spain but Federer is from Switzerland.

    B. Nadal plays better in the tennis court built of clay，while Federer plays better in the tennis court built of grass and concrete.

    C. Federer has seven Grand Slams on hard courts，while Nadal has none.

    D. All the above.

( ) 2. What kind of the tennis court is it in Wimbledon Championships(锦标赛)？

    A. Clay court.   B. Grass court.

    C. Concrete court.   D. The passage doesn't tell us.

( ) 3. What kind of the tennis court is it in French Opens?

    A. Clay court.   B. Grass court.

    C. Concrete court.   D. The passage doesn't tell us.

( ) 4. Where was Nadal's most recent win according to the passage?

    A. French Opens.   B. Australia Opens.

    C. Wimbledon Championships.   D. The Monte Carlo Masters.

( ) 5. Why does the passage say that Nadal has won 98 out of his last 99 matches on clay?

    A. Because he missed one of the 99 matches.

    B. Because he lost to Federer in the match in 2007 and that was the only flaw in his clay court record.

    C. Because he had a kind of serious illness so he couldn't take part in the match in 2007.

    D. The passage doesn't tell us the reason.

20

Liu limps(跛行) off to a trail(痕迹) of tears

A false start, a hobble(跛行，一瘸一拐地走) and the face of China's athletics(体育运动，尤指跑和跳) walked away from the Bird's Nest, <u>shattering billions of people's dream.</u>

Liu Xiang entered the track(跑道) to cheers from flag-waving fans around 11：45 am. He took off his track jacket and walked to his lane(赛道，跑道). It was the last heats(预赛) of the first round(轮) of the men's 110m hurdles(跨栏比赛).

Liu walked with a slight(轻微的) limp but stretched(伸长) out his right leg, slipped into(拖着脚步走过去) his position and ran—but in pain—when there was a false start.

He then stood up and walked away in silence(沉默). The reason：injury(伤) in the

Achilles tendon(跟腱). He was too heartbroken(极其伤心的) to emerge(出现) in public again during the day.

There was silence and tears in the National Stadium, filled to a capacity of 90 000 spectators.

The shock(震惊) was all round. Disbelief, choked(愤怒的) voices and damp(潮湿的) eyes were the order of the moment. People who had gathered to watch the first appearance of their sports icon(圣人) were numb(麻木的) for words.

A couple from Qingdao sat alone in the stadium, refusing(拒绝) to leave even an hour after Liu's race had ended. They had small Chinese national flags stuck in their hair and red hearts painted on their faces. "I can't believe it," said the woman, "I hope he would return soon." Volunteers(志愿者) finally persuaded(劝说) the couple to leave later.

But there was hope too, especially in Vice-President(副主席) Xi Jinping's telegram(电报) to the General Administration of Sport(国家体育总局) to sympathize(同情) for Liu's pullout(退出). State leaders are worried over his injury but hope he will recover(恢复)soon, Xi said, encouraging(鼓励) Liu and his coach(教练) Sun Haiping not to lose heart.

"We hope he will take proper rest and focus on his recovery. We hope that after he recovers, he will continue to train hard and struggle(奋斗) harder for national glory(荣誉)."

Liu said he would cooperate with(与……合作) doctors and try to return to the tracks as soon as possible.

Why is Liu Xiang so important? He is the first Chinese, indeed the first Asian man, to win a gold in an Olympic track event(径赛). He proved(证明) his Athens win was no flash in the pan(昙花一现) by bettering the world record later. And he had the chance to defend(卫冕) his title at home.

The ace hurdler(王牌跨栏选手) outlined his plan for the next four years after winning the gold in 2004. His was a plan with its route clearly mapped out. A gold in the 110m hurdles final at the Bird's Nest on Thursday night was his goal(目标)—and that of China's 1.3 billion people.

He may return to the London Olympics in 2012. He may regain(重新获得) the world record. Or, he could win the world title next year. But neither he nor anyone else can make up for(补偿) Monday's loss(损失).

Feng Shuyong, head coach of China's athletics team, however, said at a press conference(新闻发布会): "Liu has a strong will(毅力) fight till the last minute if his injury hadn't been so serious(严重的), he would never have withdrawn(退出) from the race."

Liu's coach Sun Haiping, who broke down（痛哭）at the press conference, explained（解释）that the hurdler suffered an injury in the Achilles' tendon more than six years ago but it worsened（加重）during training on Saturday.

"Liu's heel（脚后跟）bone is different from others and so his Achilles' tendon is more vulnerable（易受伤的）, but we had taken care of the pain properly before. It didn't hurt him till Saturday," Sun said.

"Liu insisted on（坚持）running at the Beijing Games. Before the warming up（热身运动）for the race, three doctors tried their best to ease（缓解）the pain but it didn't subside（消失）. Even then Liu decided to run, risking（拿……冒险）his career.

Feng, who said he was the "best witness（证人）of the painful road Liu had undertaken", praised（赞扬）the hurdler for his strong mind（意志）and positive spirit（积极的精神）. "Liu was in very good form（状态）before Saturday."

His strongest rival（对手）and current（现在的）world record holder, Cuba's Dayron Robles, regretted（表示遗憾）the loss of his rival in the competition.

"I'm sorry for him," Robles told China Daily, "because he is a big athlete, and a big rival for everybody. He is a good man." Robles, who broke（打破）Liu's world record in June, cruised into（进入）the second round of the heats by finishing first earlier in the day.

Choose the right answer：

（　　）1. What does the phrase "shattering billions of people's dream" mean in the passage?

A. Make billions of people lose hope.

B. Make billions of people's dream come true.

C. Make billions of people have a new dream.

D. Make billions of people excited.

（　　）2. How many spectators went to watch Liu's race in National Stadium?

A. 90 000. 　　　　　　　　　 B. 100 000.

C. 11 450. 　　　　　　　　　 D. The passage doesn't tell us.

（　　）3. According to the passage, what was the public's reaction（回应，反应）to Liu's withdrawal from the race（退赛）?

A. All the people didn't pay attention to Liu.

B. Some were shocked, some disbelieved it, some were angry, some were sad, and others were understanding and still hopeful of Liu.

C. All the people still supported Liu.

D. All the people were extremely angry and disappointed.

（　　）4. Why is Liu Xiang so important to Chinese?

A. Because he is the first Chinese and the first Asian man to win a gold in an

Olympic track event.

    B. Because he proved his Athens win was no flash in the pan by bettering the world record later.

    C. Because he had the chance to defend his title in Beijing Olympic Games.

    D. All the above.

(   ) 5. What was Robles' reaction to Liu's withdrawal?

    A. He was very happy because a strong rival had gone.

    B. He didn't care about Liu's situation.

    C. He was sorry for Liu because he thought Liu was a big athlete, a big rival for everybody, and a very good man.

    D. He was so sad that he also withdrew from the race.

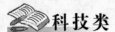 科技类

范文解析

    Water is the "life blood" of our earth. It is in every living thing. It is in the air. It runs through mountains and valleys. It forms lakes and seas. Nature has a great water system. Rainwater finds its way to rivers and lakes. River water runs into the sea. At the mouths of the rivers, fresh water joins the salt water of the sea.

    Here at the mouth of a river there is much important plant and animal life. But pollution destroys this life. We have to clean our rivers. Man has to work with nature, not against it.

Choose the right answer:

(   ) 1. Water is like _____.

    A. clouds   B. blood   C. rain   D. life

(   ) 2. _____ is in every living thing.

    A. Blood   B. Water   C. Salt   D. Air

(   ) 3. The mouth of a river is near _____.

    A. the sea   B. a lake

    C. a mountain   D. a valley

(   ) 4. There is much plant and animal life at the _____ of a river.

    A. head   B. top   C. mouth   D. foot

(   ) 5. We have to _____ our rivers.

    A. find   B. use   C. pollute   D. clean

【答案与解析】

1. **B** 可由文章第一句 "Water is the 'life blood' of our earth." 得知。水是我们地球

上的"生命血液",因此得知本文将水比作血液。要注意关键词是 blood,而不是 life,所以在选择时注意不要错选成 D。还要注意此题题干中的 like 是介词,意思是"像……一样",不要错误地理解成"喜欢"。

2. **B**　可由文章第二句 "It is in every living thing."得知。此句中的 it 根据上下文明显是指前文中已经提到的 water。

3. **A**　可由第一段最后一句 "At the mouths of the rivers, fresh water joins the salt water of the sea."得知。此句中的 mouth 应理解成"河口",因此整句意思为"在河流的河口处,河流中新鲜的水和海洋中含有盐分的水汇聚到了一起。"由此可以推断,河流的河口处必然是靠近海洋的,这样河水才有可能与海水汇聚起来。

4. **C**　可由第二段第一句 "Here at the mouth of a river there is much important plant and animal life."直接得知。

5. **D**　可由第二段中的两句话 "But pollution destroys this life. We have to clean our rivers."直接得知。

实战演练

1

Air is all around us. It is around us as we walk and play. From the time we were born air is around us on every side. When we sit down, it is around us. When we go to bed, air is also around us. We live in air. We can live without food or water for a few days, but we cannot live for more than a few minutes without air. We take in air. When we are working or running, we need more air. When we are asleep, we need less air.

We live in air, but we cannot see it. We can only feel it. We can feel it when it is moving. Moving air is called wind. How can we make air move? Here is one way. Hold an open book in front of your face, close it quickly. What can you feel? What you feel is air.

True or False:

(　　) 1. When we are asleep, we need no air.

(　　) 2. We cannot live without air for more than a few minutes.

(　　) 3. We cannot see air.

(　　) 4. Wind is moving air.

(　　) 5. We can neither see nor feel air.

2

Life on the earth depends on the sun. Day after day we see its light and feel its warmth. The sun is far away from the earth. It is ninety-three million miles away from the earth.

The sun is a large star. The earth is very small among its planets. Every day the sun sends out a great deal of heat and makes us feel hot. But we receive only a small part of the heat, because the sun is so far away from us and its heat loses more of its energy when it reaches the earth. We also receive a very small part of its light. This is enough for the growth of trees, plants, and humans. On the other hand, much heat and light would be harmful to them. The heat and light from the sun come in just the right quantities for life on the earth.

True or False:

(　　) 1. Without the sun, there would be no living things on the earth.

(　　) 2. The earth is the smallest of all the planets of the sun.

(　　) 3. We only receive a small part of light from the sun. The light is not enough for trees and plants to grow on the earth.

(　　) 4. Much heat and light would be good for the living things on the earth.

(　　) 5. Every day a lot of heat is given off to the earth by the sun.

3

The computer is fast, and never makes a mistake, while people are too slow and full of mistakes sometimes. That's what people often say when they talk about computers. For over a quarter of a century, engineers have been making better and better computers. Now a computer can do a lot of everyday jobs wonderfully. It is widely used in factories, hospitals, banks and universities. A computer can report, decide and control in almost every field. Many computer scientists are now thinking of making the computer "think" like a man. With the help of a person, a computer can draw pictures, write music, talk with people, play chess, recognize voices, translate languages and so on. Perhaps computers will one day really think and feel. Do you think people will be afraid when they find that the computer is too clever to listen to and serve the people?

True or False:

(　　) 1. People often say that the computer never makes a mistake while people often make mistakes.

(　　) 2. For over a century, engineers have been making better and better computers.

(　　) 3. Now a computer can do a lot of everyday jobs well.

(　　) 4. The computer has been widely used in factories, hospitals, banks, universities and hotels.

(　　) 5. The computer will certainly take the place of people one day.

4

There is nothing more important to life than the sun. Without the sun all living things on the earth would die.

The sun is a star. In the sky there are thousands of stars like the sun. They are as large as the sun and as hot as the sun. At night you can see many stars，but in the day-time you can only see one star—the sun.

The sun is much nearer to us than any other star. That is why it looks the biggest and brightest of all the stars. The distance of the sun from the earth is as much as 150 million kilometres. Most of the stars are thousands of light years away from the earth.

Do you know the light year? Nothing in the world travels faster than light. It travels 300 000 kilometres a second. And one light year is the distance that light travels in one year.

Choose the right answer：

(　) 1. _____ can live without the sun.

　　A. People　　　B. Animals　　　C. Plants　　　D. Nothing

(　) 2. The most important to life is _____ .

　　A. the moon　　B. the stars　　C. the sun　　D. the sky

(　) 3. The sun looks the biggest and brightest of all the stars because _____ .

　　A. it's the biggest of all the stars

　　B. it's the brightest of all the stars

　　C. it's much nearer to us than any other star

　　D. it's far away from the earth

(　) 4. Light travels _____ in the world.

　　A. fastest　　　B. slowest　　　C. much faster　　D. much slower

(　) 5. From the passage we know that light travels _____ kilometres per minute.

　　A. 600 000　　　B. 300 000　　　C. 150 000　　　D. 18 000 000

5

We all live on the earth. The earth turns around once a day. As it turns, some people see sunrise and day comes to their houses；at the same time other people see sunset and night comes to their houses.

The earth moves in another way，too. If it travels around the sun in an orbit towards the sun, it is summer on that part of the earth. Half a year later, the earth goes round to the other side of its orbit. That part of the earth is now farther away from the sun and has its winter，and the other part has its summer. Between summer and winter, both halves of the earth are the same distance from the sun. Then they have spring and autumn. As the earth goes round in its orbit, we have our four seasons go on and on.

Choose the right answer：

(   ) 1. We can see sunrise and sunset because _____ .

     A. the sun is near to us

     B. the earth turns around once a day

     C. the sun goes out of the clouds in the daytime and into them at night

     D. the earth moves round the sun

(   ) 2. There are four seasons in a year because _____ .

     A. the earth moves round the sun

     B. the sun turns round the earth

     C. the sun moves from one place to another

     D. the earth travels nearer and nearer to the sun

(   ) 3. When the earth goes round the sun, we have _____ on the part that is towards the sun.

     A. spring   B. summer   C. autumn   D. winter

(   ) 4. When we have winter, the part of the earth that we stand on is _____ .

     A. near the sun

     B. nearer to the sun

     C. farther away from the sun

     D. the same distance as the other part from it

(   ) 5. When both halves of the earth are the same distance from the sun, we have _____ .

     A. spring and autumn   B. spring and winter

     C. summer and winter   D. summer and autumn

6

Here is a good idea for future cars. There will be electronic tracks everywhere in the streets. Electronic cars will run on these tracks. All the tracks and all the cars will be controlled by a great computer. For example, if you want to go from your school to a large factory, you just go out of the school and get into one of those cars outside. Then you press the button for the factory. A signal is sent from the car to the central computer and the computer finds the route. The car takes you to the factory at high speed. Easy!

Don't you think it is a good idea for the future? If we really want to realize it, we must do something, we do not want to live in noisy, dirty cities, do we?

Choose the right answer：

(   ) 1. Electronic tracks will be used _____ .

     A. in the street   B. in cities

C. in large factories   D. in the country

(   ) 2. _____ leads the car to the place you want to go.

     A. The electronic tracks   B. The button

     C. The signal   D. The central computer

(   ) 3. The idea of electronic tracks _____.

     A. can never be realized

     B. can be realized if people do something

     C. can only be realized in large factories

     D. is realized everywhere

(   ) 4. The computer gets signal from _____

     A. schools   B. factories

     C. electronic cars   D. electronic tracks

(   ) 5. When you want to go to a place, just press a button _____.

     A. outside the car   B. in the car

     C. on the computer   D. in the factory

7

Scientists are trying to make the deserts into good land again. They want to bring water to the deserts, so people can live and grow food. They are learning a lot about the deserts. But more and more of the earth is becoming deserts all the time. Scientists may not be able to change the desert in time.

Why is more and more land becoming deserts? Scientists think that people make deserts. People are doing bad things to the earth.

Some places on the earth don't get very much rain. But they still don't become deserts. This is because some green plants are growing there. Small green plants and grass are very important to dry places. Plants don't let the hot sun make the earth even drier. Plants don't let the wind blow the dirt away. When a little bit of rain falls, the plants hold the water. Without plants, the land can become a desert much more easily.

Choose the right answer:

(   ) 1. Deserts _____.

     A. get very little rain

     B. never have any plants or animals in them

     C. can all be turned into good land before long

     D. both A and C

(   ) 2. Small green plants are very important to dry places because _____.

     A. they don't let the sun make the earth even drier

     B. they don't let the wind blow the earth away

C. they hold water

D. all of the above

(   ) 3. Land is becoming deserts little by little because _____.

       A. plants can't grow there

       B. there is not enough rain

       C. people are doing bad things to the earth

       D. scientists know little about the deserts

(   ) 4. Which is the main idea of the first paragraph?

       A. Scientists know how to change deserts into good land.

       B. Land is becoming desert faster than scientists can change it back into good land.

       C. If scientists can bring water to desert, people can live and grow food there.

       D. More and more places are becoming deserts all the time.

(   ) 5. After reading this, we learn that _____.

       A. plants can keep dry land from becoming deserts

       B. it is good to get rid of the grass in the deserts

       C. all places without much rain will become deserts

       D. it is better to grow crops on dry land than to grow grass

8

Robots are becoming a big part of our lives. There may be half a million robots in the USA 20 years from now.

These machines are changing the way work is being done. Thousands of robots are used in factories. These robots are not like the robots in movies. They don't walk or talk. Instead, a robot may be just a metal arm. The robot arm can do a certain job in a factory over and over again. It can do jobs that people may not want to do. A robot never gets tired of doing the same thing.

Sometimes a robot gets to do more exciting work. In Canada, police are using a robot on wheels. This robot's job is to take apart(去除) bombs that may go off(爆炸).

Choose the right answer:

(   ) 1. Robots are becoming _____.

       A. more and more important   B. less important than before

       C. useless   D. more and more expensive

(   ) 2. Robots can _____.

       A. walk in the factories

       B. do a certain job in a factory over and over again

       C. talk with people

D. get tired of doing the same job

(　　) 3. A title for the story could be _____.

　　A. Robot's Job　　　　　　B. Jobs in the Factories

　　C. Robots on Wheels　　　D. Robots in Our Lives

(　　) 4. Robots in Canada can probably _____.

　　A. build a bomb　B. make films　C. save lives　D. walk and talk

(　　) 5. What are the robots used in factories like according to the passage?

　　A. They are just like the robots in movies.

　　B. They can walk fast and talk to people.

　　C. They can have the same feeling as people.

　　D. They may be just some metal arms which can do certain jobs in a factory over and over again and which never get tired of doing the same thing.

9

One summer day a raindrop fell from a cloud. Many other raindrops fell at the same time, but our story is about just one raindrop.

The raindrop fell to the ground on the side of a hill. The water in the raindrop ran down the hill into a little river. The little river carried the raindrop to a big river. Then the raindrop travelled far to the east into the sea. There the water of the raindrop mixed itself with the salt water of the sea.

Now the water of the raindrop was on the surface of the sea. As the sun made it very warm, it changed into steam. The steam left the sea and went up into the air, and it did not carry any salt with it. It had left the salt in the sea.

The steam from the raindrop moved with the warm air towards the north. On the way the warm air met some cold. The cold air pushed the warm air high above the ground. The warm air became cool when it went up, and the steam in it changed into very small drops of water again. There were millions and millions of these small drops in the cloud. The small drops came together into bigger and bigger drops. Our raindrop was one of them. Now the drop became so big that it was too heavy to stay in the cloud, and it fell to the ground. In this way the water of our raindrop，started travelling to the sea again.

Choose the right answer：

(　　) 1. The story is about _____.

　　A. cloud　　　B. rain　　　C. water　　　D. a raindrop

(　　) 2. The water of the raindrop mixed itself with the salt water in _____.

　　A. the sea　　B. a big river　C. a little river　D. lake

(　　) 3. The water of the raindrop went up into the air from the sea _____.

A. without salt when it changed into steam

B. with salt when it changed into steam

C. without salt before it changed into steam

D. with salt after it changed into steam

(　　) 4. The small water drops in the cloud fell down because _____.

A. there were millions and millions of them in the cloud

B. the sea wanted to take them back

C. they wanted to start travelling on the ground again

D. they became so heavy that the cloud couldn't hold them up any longer

(　　) 5. Why did the raindrop change into the steam?

A. Because the raindrop was on the surface of the sea.

B. Because the water of the raindrop mixed itself with the salt water of the sea.

C. Because as the raindrop was on the surface of the sea, the sun made it very warm, so soon the raindrop lost its water and it became the steam.

D. Because the raindrop moved with the warm air towards the north.

10

There have been many great inventions, things that changed the way we live. The first great invention was one that is still very important today—the wheel. This made it easier to carry heavy things and to travel long distances.

For hundreds of years after that there were few inventions that had as much effect as the wheel. Then in the early 1800s the world started to change. There was little unknown land left in the world. People didn't have to explore much any more. They began to work instead to make life better.

In the second half of the 19th century many great inventions were made. Among them were the camera, the light and the radio. These all became a big part of our life today.

The first part of the 20th century saw more great inventions. The helicopter in 1909. Movies with sound in 1926. The computer in 1928. And jet planes in 1930. This was also a time when a new material was first made. Nylon came out in 1935. It changed the kind of clothes people wear.

The middle part of the 20th century brought new ways to help people get over diseases. They worked very well. They made people healthier and let them live longer. By the 1960s most people could expect to live to be at least 60.

By this time most people had a very good life. Of course new inventions continued to be made. But man now had a desire to explore again. The world was known to man but the stars were not. Man began looking for ways to go into space. Russia made the first step. Then the United States took a step. Since then other countries, including China and Japan, have made their steps into space.

In 1969 man took his biggest step away from earth. Americans first walked on the moon. This is certainly just a beginning. New inventions will some day allow us to do things we have never yet dreamed of.

Choose the right answer:

(　　) 1. This passage talks mainly about _____.

    A. why cars were very important

    B. when light was invented

    C. which country made the first step into space

    D. how inventions affect people's life

(　　) 2. In 1800s, people began to work in order to make _____.

    A. explorations　　　　　　B. life better

    C. discoveries　　　　　　　D. a trip to space

(　　) 3. Nylon came out nearly at the same time as _____.

    A. radio　　　　B. camera　　　　C. jet planes　　　　D. movies

(　　) 4. People can live longer lives because _____ to help people cure diseases have worked very well.

    A. doctors　　　　B. new ways　　　　C. medicines　　　　D. new hospitals

(　　) 5. Man didn't have a desire to explore a lot _____.

    A. at the beginning of 1800s　　　　B. in 1960s

    C. since 1900s　　　　　　　　　　D. from 1800s to 1960s

11

Space is not black, but light green, a team of astronomers said on January 10th. They studied the light sent out by 200 000 galaxies. What they found was that the colour of the space is a bit greener than turquoise(绿宝石).

The discovery was part of an attempt to test theories(理论) about how stars and galaxies form.

Most astronomers believe that the space maybe started with a "blue period" when young blue stars filled space. Now the universe is in a "green period". They believe it will finally enter a "red period" when the older redder stars appear.

"The reason for the colour changing is that the rate of stars forming is changing." said Ivan Baldry, an astronomer who worked to find the colour of light in the space.

There is no way any human could actually see the green colour.

"The only way to see it is only if you saw the whole space from the same distance away and it was not moving," Baldry said.

Choose the right answer：

(   ) 1. From the passage, we know there _____ for us to actually see the green colour in the space.

       A. is only one way   B. is no way

       C. are two ways   D. are three ways

(   ) 2. What did the space start with as most astronomers believe?

       A. Blue period when young red stars filled space.

       B. Blue period when old blue stars filled space.

       C. Blue period when young blue stars filled space.

       D. Blue period when old red stars filled space.

(   ) 3. What is the reason for the colour changing?

       A. The rate of colours forming is changing.

       B. The rate of space forming is changing.

       C. The rate of stars forming is changing.

       D. The rate of periods forming is changing.

(   ) 4. After the green period, the space might enter _____ finally.

       A. a red period   B. a yellow period

       C. a blue period   D. a black period

(   ) 5. How many periods of space are mentioned in the passage?

       A. Four.   B. Three.   C. Two.   D. One.

12

Many animals do strange things before an earthquake. This news may be important. Earthquakes can kill people and knock down houses. The animals may help to save lives.

Some animals make a lot of noise before an earthquake. Farmers have told about this. Dogs that are usually quiet have started to bark. Horses on farms have run around in circles. Mice have left their holes and run away. Cows have given less milk.

In a town in Italy, cats raced down the street in a group. That happened only a few hours before an earthquake. In San Francisco, a man kept tiny pet frogs. One Sunday, the frogs jumped around more than ever. They made loud noises, like bigger frogs. That night, an earthquake struck the city.

People want to know when an earthquake is coming. Then they could get away safely. Right now, there is no sure way to know an earthquake ahead of time. Maybe the best idea is to watch the animals.

Choose the right answer：

(   ) 1. This story is mostly about _____.

A. how animals act before an earthquake

B. how an earthquake starts

C. how mice leave their holes

D. how frogs make loud noises

(　　) 2. The passage tells us that before an earthquake, quiet dogs _____.

    A. ran away   B. started to bark

    C. climbed trees   D. raced down the street

(　　) 3. The passage tells us that before the earthquake, the frogs _____.

    A. sang

    B. left their homes

    C. jumped around a lot and made loud noises

    D. ran around in circles

(　　) 4. According to(根据) the passage, there have been earthquakes in _____.

    A. all the countries in the world   B. Italy and San Francisco

    C. Chicago and Spain   D. Britain and the USA

(　　) 5. People want to _____.

    A. be in the earthquake

    B. find out early about an earthquake

    C. run around in circles

    D. stop all the earthquakes from happening

13

In Britain the weather never gets too hot or too cold. There is not a great difference between summer and winter. Why is this?

Britain has a warm winter and a cool summer because it is an island country. In winter the sea is warmer than the land. The winds from the sea bring warm air to Britain. In summer the sea is cooler than the land. The winds from the sea bring cool air to Britain.

The winds from the west blow over Britain all the year. They blow from the southwest across the Atlantic Ocean. They are wet winds. They bring rain to Britain all the year. Britain has a lot of rain all the year. The west of Britain is wetter than the east. The winds must blow across the high land in the west. The east of Britain is drier than the west.

Choose the right answer:

(　　) 1. What's the weather like in Britain?

    A. It's either too hot or too cold.

    B. It's both too hot and too cold.

C. It's neither too hot nor too cold.

D. We don't know.

(   ) 2. When do the winds bring cool air to Britain?

    A. In spring.   B. In summer.

    C. In autumn.   D. In winter.

(   ) 3. Why is the weather in summer and in winter almost the same in Britain?

    A. There is no difference between summer and winter in Britain.

    B. There is sea air around this country.

    C. There are winds from the high land.

    D. There is much rain in the Atlantic Ocean.

(   ) 4. Which of the following is right?

    A. There is more rain in the east than in the west.

    B. There is as much rain in the west as in the east.

    C. There is less rain in the east than in the west.

    D. There isn't so much rain in the west as in the east.

(   ) 5. The passage tells us _____.

    A. the seasons in Britain   B. the rain in Britain

    C. the weather in Britain   D. the winds in Britain

14

NASA's Mars rover(探测器), Spirit, was in good health as it made its way into space. Spirit is going to see whether there is life on the Red Planet. The rover was sent into space on June 10th from Florida, USA. The 311 million-mile trip is expected to take seven months. NASA plans to launch another rover, Opportunity, at the end of June. Weeks ago, the European Space Agency's Mars Express took off from Russia with the same task of finding out whether there is life on Mars.

True or False：

(   ) 1. The condition of Spirit was good when it was sent into space.

(   ) 2. Spirit is expected to take seven weeks to finish the trip.

(   ) 3. Spirit is going to Moon to see if there is life on the planet.

(   ) 4. Opportunity is the name of another rover.

(   ) 5. The European Space Agency will send another rover at the end of June.

15

Wearing the wrong type of glasses will do harm to your eyes. This is not true for adults, although incorrect glasses may not be good for children under 10.

Ready-made(现成的) glasses, and not wearing when you should, won't do harm to your eyes, but you may see better with glasses that are specially made for you.

Watching too much television is bad for your eyes. This is not true. People with easily affected(感染) eyes may find they get red and aching(疼痛的) from staring(盯) at a fixed distance for a long time, but it won't last long.

Carrots will help you see in the dark. Carrots are rich in beta-carotene(胡萝卜素), which the body can change into Vitamin A, too little of which can cause night blindness. However, people in most countries don't need to worry about Vitamin A deficiency(缺乏). Night blindness is more likely to be connected with another vision problem.

Choose the right answer:

(　　) 1. Which of the following is true?

A. Ready-made glasses will do harm to our eyes.

B. Wearing the wrong glasses may do harm to children's eyes.

C. Our bodies are unable to change beta-carotene into Vitamin A.

D. Watching less television may do harm to children's eyes.

(　　) 2. Watching too much television can cause _____.

A. night blindness　　　　　　B. lasting eye problems

C. a number of vision problems　D. eye trouble for a time

(　　) 3. You can see better by _____.

A. wearing specially-made glasses　B. doing eye exercises

C. cutting back on television　　　D. eating more carrots

(　　) 4. Night blindness is most likely caused by _____.

A. staring for a long time　　　B. too much beta-carotene

C. the loss of Vitamin A　　　　D. a vision problem

(　　) 5. The main purpose of this passage is to tell us _____.

A. the importance of our eyes　　B. how to protect our eyes

C. to have more carrots　　　　　D. something more about our eyes

16

If you dream of becoming a spaceman after you grow up, get started now! A spaceman needs a strong body and mind. See here what Shenzhou Ⅵ spacemen are able to do. Do you still have a long way to go?

Shenzhou Ⅵ spacemen are able to live upside down(头朝下地). They do this not just during sleep, but also when eating and going to the toilet. Before they flew into space, they had lots of practice. Each upside-down training time lasted for 20 days.

In Shenzhou Ⅵ, Chinese spacemen aren't just spaceship drivers but also machine repairers and scientists. They have to know every part of the spaceship and how it works. If something goes wrong, they must know how to repair it. Also they do scientific experiments in space.

Shenzhou Ⅵ spacemen know how to live in the wild. They took a knife, a gun and some dye(染料) with them into space. If they land in forests, the knife and gun can protect them from wild animals. If they fall into the sea, the dye can colour the sea water around them yellow. This can help people find them easily on the sea.

Shenzhou Ⅵ spacemen can't get dizzy. A spaceship is not a plane. When it goes up, the extra gravity force(重力) can break people's bones. Spacemen must have strong bodies for this. They can't get a headache or be sick. With many things to take care of, they've got no time for sickness.

Choose the right answer:

(　　) 1. That the writer says "get started now if you want to be a spaceman" means _____.

      A. you have to train your body and work hard at your studies when you are young

      B. young men have many dreams

      C. only young men have many dreams

      D. young men can drive a spaceship

(　　) 2. It took _____ for Shenzhou Ⅵ spacemen to do each upside-down training.

      A. 20 months   B. 20 days   C. 20 years   D. a month

(　　) 3. Shenzhou Ⅵ spacemen took some dye with them into space to _____.

      A. colour their hair if they have free time

      B. colour something in an experiment

      C. protect them from wild animals if they land in forests

      D. help people find them easily if they fall into the sea

(　　) 4. Which of the following is NOT true to Shenzhou Ⅵ spacemen?

      A. They are able to stand on their heads.

      B. They can drive the spaceship and repair it.

      C. They are so busy that they get sick.

      D. They have some scientific experiments in space.

(　　) 5. The best title of the passage may be _____.

      A. A Story about Space

      B. How to Sleep in Space

      C. Spacemen Need Special Training

      D. Anyone Can Drive a Spaceship

17

Scientists wanted to know more about the universe. They thought the best way was to send men to space. Man has landed on the moon successfully. The moon is about 384 000 kilometres away from Earth. A plane cannot fly to space because the air reaches only 240 kilometres away from Earth. But something can fly even when there is no air. That's a rocket. A rocket can send a spacecraft into space. How does a rocket fly? There is gas in the rocket. When the gas inside the rocket got hot enough, it will rush out of the end of the rocket, so it can make the rocket fly up into the sky. Rockets can fly far out into space. Spacecraft without <u>astronauts</u> in them have been to Mars. It's farther from us than the moon is. Scientists hope to find a planet like Earth in space.

Choose the right answer:

( ) 1. How far is it from Earth to the moon?

      A. 240 kilometres.   B. 384 000 kilometres.

      C. 2 005 kilometres.   D. 22 000 kilometres.

( ) 2. _____ can take people into space.

      A. Planes   B. Planets   C. Air   D. Spacecraft

( ) 3. The hot gas in the rocket is used for _____.

      A. keeping the rocket warm

      B. cooking delicious food for astronauts

      C. making the rocket fly into space

      D. making the moon warm

( ) 4. What does the underlined word "astronauts" mean in the passage?

      A. 宇航员   B. 飞行员   C. 科学家   D. 驾驶员

( ) 5. Which of the following is NOT wrong?

      A. Japanese have been to the moon.

      B. Scientists found another "Earth" in space.

      C. Chinese astronauts have landed safely on the moon.

      D. Spacecraft without men in them have been to another planet of the sun's family.

18

Robots are smart. With their computer brains, they help people work in dangerous places or do different jobs. Bobby, the robot mail carrier, brings mails to a large office building in Washington DC He is one of 250 robot mail carriers in the United States. There is also Mr Leachim, the robot fourth-grade teacher.

Mr Leachim, who weighs two hundred pounds and is six feet tall, has some advantages(优点) as a teacher. One advantage is that he doesn't forget details. He knows each child's name, the parents' names, and what each child knows and needs to know. In addition, he knows each child's pets and hobbies. Mr Leachim doesn't make mistakes. Each child goes to tell his or her name, then dial(拨) an identification number. His computer brain puts the child's voice and number together. He identifies (识别)the child with no mistakes. Then he starts the lesson.

Another advantage is that Mr Leachim is flexible(灵活的). If the children need more time to do their lessons they can move switches(转换器). In this way they can repeat Mr Leachim's lesson over and over again. When the children do a good job, he tells them something interesting about their hobbies. At the end of the lesson the children switch Mr Leachim off.

Choose the right answer：

( ) 1. Robots _____.

    A. can help people do easy jobs   B. can help people do different jobs

    C. only carry mails   D. are not intelligent

( ) 2. Mr Leachim is a _____.

    A. mail carrier robot   B. fourth-grade teacher

    C. robot fourth-grade teacher   D. the inventor of a robot

( ) 3. Mr Leachim has _____ as a teacher.

    A. some advantages   B. no advantages

    C. one hobby   D. no hobbies

( ) 4. When you can name somebody, or tell who somebody is, you can _____ that person.

    A. improve   B. admit

    C. persuade   D. identify

( ) 5. Which of the following statements is TRUE according to the passage?

    A. Bobby is a robot mail carrier in an office building.

    B. Mr Leachim identifies a child by his or her voice only.

    C. There are 250 robot mail carriers in the United States.

    D. When the lesson is over, the child dials an identification.

19

The many moons of Jupiter travel around the planet in different directions.

Jupiter is the largest planet in our solar system. Over the years, scientists have found that Jupiter has its own small solar system. Earth has one moon. Jupiter has at least sixteen and probably more.

Since there are so many moons, scientists began to number them. The numerals (numbers) tell the sequence, or order, in which the moons were found. They were slower to name the moons. All of Jupiter's moons now have a name as well as a number.

The first five moons to be discovered are known as the "inner moons". But they are not the closest to the planet. The closest is only 127 600 kilometres away from Jupiter. All the inner moons circle the planet in counter-clockwise direction, that is, opposite of the hands of a clock.

Jupiter's middle group of moons are at least 11 100 000 kilometres from the planet. They also move in a counter-clockwise motion(moving). The four farthest moons are at least 20 700 000 kilometres away. These are called "outer moons". They circle in a clockwise motion.

How many more moons do you think will be discovered?

Choose the right answer:

( ) 1. What does "solar system" in this article mean?

    A. 银河系   B. 宇宙空间

    C. 流星雨   D. 太阳系

( ) 2. Things that travel in the same direction as the hands of a clock are said to be traveling in a _____ .

    A. clockwise direction   B. counter-clockwise direction

    C. same direction   D. different direction

( ) 3. Jupiter's _____ group of moons travel in a clockwise direction.

    A. planets   B. inner   C. middle   D. outer

( ) 4. The numbers given to Jupiter's moons tell _____ .

    A. the order in which they were discovered

    B. the order in which they travel

    C. the order of their distance from Jupiter

    D. the order of the names

( ) 5. According to the passage, which of the following statements is TRUE?

    A. None of Jupiter's moons have names.

    B. Most of Jupiter's moons circle clockwise.

    C. Jupiter's inner moons were discovered first.

    D. Jupiter is the nearest planet to the earth.

20

Matt Mason has seen the future—and it's fun. Mason likes thinking about how machines can make our lives easier by doing the work we hate, such as cleaning. He shows a hard floor cleaning system that's built into the wall: it will blow dirt to a part of the room where it will be collected by a vacuum(吸尘器). Then the system will drop some cleaner on the floor and an arm will mop(用拖把拖) it up. "This may trouble you," says Kara, an expert in Mason's company. "But you can program it to come on at 3 am, and it will just wet-mop the floor for you."

When it comes to the kitchen, Bruce Beihoff, another expert at Whirlpool, is sure that in a few years, robots will be doing most of the boring work, freeing us to relax. "More than just fun, future kitchens will be environmentally friendly," he says. "A new system will be built in the house which can recycle energy lost from your kitchen to make the whole home warm."

"The fridge will be the centre of the home," says Daniel Lee, a market expert. The fridge will have a touch screen where you can watch TV, surf the Internet, check your e-mails, keep a shopping list and order vegetables. "Your fridge is the first place you go in the morning and the last place at night," says Lee.

Ever wonder why a 1.9-metre man and a 1.6-metre woman have to cook meals on counters(工作台) of the same height. "The height was decided over 50 years ago, according to the height of ordinary women," says Jane Langmuir, an expert of cooking machines. "But times have changed. We have made a new counter where you press a button and it moves to whatever height you want." At the same time, Ted Selker at MIT's counter lab has made the dishmaker, which lets you make dishes, and bowls out of plastics at home. After each meal, the dishes are changed straight back into plastics.

Choose the right answer:

(   ) 1. How many inventions are mentioned in the passage?

       A. Three.   B. Four.   C. Five.   D. Six.

(   ) 2. In the future, if you want to clean your house, you will _____.

       A. have a recycling system built in the wall

       B. get up early to start your cleaning system

       C. use your fridge to give orders to a cleaner

       D. leave the work to a kind of cleaning machine

(   ) 3. What's future kitchen work like?

       A. Terrible and boring.   B. Easy and interesting.

       C. Enjoyable and excited.   D. Funny and amazing.

(   ) 4. From the passage, we know _____.

       A. people will have more and more time enjoying themselves

       B. future kitchens can provide all the energy for our life every day

       C. the fridge can be found in the centre of a future house

       D. people must be expert at computers to use these inventions

(   ) 5. A new system will be built in the house which can recycle energy lost from your _____ to make the whole home warm.

       A. kitchen   B. living room

       C. the centre of the home   D. a part of the room

 应用类

✎ 范文解析

Dear Anton,

Next week I'm going to take a trip to San Francisco with my sister and her husband, and there is a seat in our car for another one. Would you like to come with us? We're going to leave on Saturday morning, February 28th and stay there for a week. All of us enjoy shopping and travelling, so we'd like to stay at a hotel called Pickwick in the centre of the town. In the day we can hike in the mountain near the town and at night go shopping together. Don't worry. You and I can have one double room.

It is about 690 kilometres from Long Beach to San Francisco, and it usually takes eight and a half hours to drive there. We are going to leave at about 6 am on Saturday so that we'll drive in the day and get there before dark. We are going to take Highway 101, so we can <u>pick you up</u> from your home in Ventura at about 8 am.

Please let me know quickly if you can come with us.

Yours,

Paul

Choose the right answer:

( ) 1. Paul writes the letter to Anton to _____.

    A. ask him to go on a trip with them

    B. ask him to do some shopping together

    C. tell him where they are going and when then are leaving

    D. tell him where Pickwick Hotel is

( ) 2. They would like to stay at Pickwick Hotel because _____.

    A. they will have fun staying in that hotel

    B. they can go shopping and hiking there more easily

    C. it is cheap to stay there

    D. it has double rooms

( ) 3. What's the meaning of the underlined phrase "pick...up"?

    A. 接　　　　B. 捡　　　　C. 搭　　　　D. 摘

( ) 4. Paul is going to pick up Anton _____.

    A. before they leave home

    B. after they get to San Francisco

    C. on their way to Long Beach

    D. on their way to San Francisco

( ) 5. How far is it from Long Beach to Ventura?

A. About 8 hours' drive.

B. About 2 hours' drive.

C. About 160 kilometres.

D. About 690 kilometres.

【答案与解析】

1. **A**　此题要注意分析写信人的目的何在。虽然信中提到了他们将去何地,何时出发,也提到了他们中途将住在一家名叫 Pickwick 的旅馆,以便游玩和购物,但这些信息都不是写信人 Paul 给 Anton 写信的根本目的。Paul 为什么要给 Anton 写信并在信中告之 Anton 上述信息,其目的是邀请 Anton 与他们一起旅行。这可以由文中第一段第二行 "Would you like to come with us?" 看出。因此在做这题时应当分析四个选项,BCD 都只是信中一些具体信息,不是写信目的,而只有 A 才是正确答案。

2. **B**　这可由文章第一段中 "All of us enjoy shopping and travelling, so we'd like to stay at a hotel called Pickwick in the centre of the town. In the day we can hike in the mountain near the town and at night go shopping together." 得知。一行人都是喜欢购物和旅行的,所以才选择居住在这家旅馆。因此可以推断,该旅馆必定是便于他们游玩和购物的,故正确答案是 B。

3. **A**　这必须根据上下文语境进行考虑。在第二段中,作者提到:"We are going to take Highway 101, so we can pick you up from your home in Ventura at about 8 am." 我们将走 101 号高速公路,这样我们可以在早晨 8 点左右在 Ventura 从你家里 "pick you up"。而第一段中写信人又提出邀请 Anton 与他们一起旅行,那么显然在这里 "pick you up" 是说接你出来,因此答案应为 A。

4. **D**　此题需要弄清楚 Paul 去接 Anton 的具体时间。仔细阅读第二段中的相应句子 "It is about 690 kilometres from Long Beach to San Francisco." 这说明他们的起点是 Long Beach,而终点是 San Francisco。那么可以知道,Paul 必定是在从 Long Beach 到 San Francisco 的路途中去接 Anton 的。"... so we can pick you up from your home in Ventura at about 8 am." 从这句可以知道,Anton 的家在 Ventura,综合上面的分析可知,Ventura 必定是在 Long Beach 和 San Francisco 之间的。他们的路线应为 Long Beach—Ventura—San Francisco。因此 Paul 是在去 San Francisco 的路上、到达 San Francisco 之前接到 Anton 的,只有 D 选项正确。

5. **B**　在第 4 题的分析中已经提到,他们的行进路线为 Long Beach—Ventura—San Francisco,而第二段中提到 "We are going to leave at about 6 am." 以及 "so we can pick you up from your home in Ventura at about 8 am." 从起点 Long Beach 出发的时间是 6 点,而到达中途 Ventura 的时间是 8 点,由此可推断,这两地之间的距离应为 two hours' drive,因此正确答案为 B。

实战演练

1

Saturday, March 24th

We have already arrived in the hot, wet city of Bangkok. This is our first trip to Thailand. All the different smells make us want to try the food. We are going to eat something special for dinner tonight. The hotel we are staying in is cheap and very clean. We plan to stay here for a few days, visit some places in the city, and then travel to Chiang Mai in the north.

Tuesday, March 27th

Bangkok is wonderful and surprising! The places are interesting. We visited the famous market which was on water, and saw a lot of fruit and vegetables. Everything is so colourful, and we have taken hundreds of photos already! Later today we will leave for Chiang Mai. We will take the train north, stay in Chiang Mai for two days, and then catch a bus to Chiang Rai.

Friday, March 30th

Our trip to Chiang Rai was long and boring. We visited a small village in the mountains. The village's people here love the quiet life—no computers or phones. They are the kindest people I have ever met. They always smile and say "hello". Kathy and I can only speak a few words of Thai, so smiling is the best way to show our kindness. I feel good here and hope to be able to come back next year.

Choose the right answer:

(　　) 1. The diaries above show the writer's _____ days in Thailand.

A. 3　　　　　　 B. 7　　　　　　 C. 15　　　　　　 D. 30

(　　) 2. It seems that visitors _____ in Bangkok.

A. often feel hungry　　　　　　 B. can always find cheap things

C. can't take any photos　　　　　　 D. can enjoy themselves

(　　) 3. Which of the following is TRUE?

A. Chiang Mai is a beautiful city in the south of Thailand.

B. The writer left Chiang Mai for Chiang Rai by bus.

C. Chiang Rai is a boring city in the mountain.

D. The writer is travelling alone in Thailand.

(　　) 4. The people in the village _____.

A. are friendly to others　　　　　　 B. like to speak English

C. are very weak　　　　　　 D. hope to live in the cities

(　　) 5. What is the best title for the whole diary?

A. My First Travel.
B. The Outside World.
C. Travelling in Thailand.
D. A Country on the Train.

2

December 25th, 2004

Dear Rose,

How are you?

I like your programmes very much. They're very interesting and I can learn a lot from them. I like travelling and I have won a free four-week trip to England, but I know little about the British way of life. Would you please write to tell me something about the British meals?

Thank you.

Yours,
Wang Lin

January 1st, 2005

Dear Wang Lin,

It's very helpful to know something about the British meals before travelling. In many English houses, people eat four meals a day. They are breakfast, lunch, afternoon tea and dinner.

Breakfast takes place at any time from 7:00 to 9:00 in the morning. They usually have eggs, bread with butter, cheese and so on. English people drink tea or coffee at breakfast. Lunch comes at one o'clock. It can be a hamburger or a three-course(三道菜的) meal. Afternoon tea is between 4:00 pm and 5:00 pm Dinner begins at about half past seven. The first course is soup. The next is often meat or fish with vegetables. Then come fruits of different kinds: apples, pears, bananas and so on. But not all English people eat like that. Some of them have their dinner in the middle of the day. Their meals are breakfast, dinner, afternoon tea and supper. And all these meals are usually simple.

Wish you a good time in England!

Yours,
Rose

Choose the right answer:

(   ) 1. Wang Lin wrote to _____.

A. say hello to Rose

B. ask Rose about the British meals

C. tell Rose about the free trip

    D. tell Rose that he liked her programmes

( ) 2. The possible time for breakfast in England is _____.

    A. from 7:00 pm to 9:00 pm B. from 7:00 am to 9:00 am

    C. from 4:00 pm to 5:00 pm D. from 4:00 am to 5:00 am

( ) 3. In England, afternoon tea often takes place _____.

    A. before lunch   B. between breakfast and lunch

    C. during supper   D. between lunch and dinner

( ) 4. The second course at dinner is often _____ at British meals.

    A. soup   B. cheese

    C. bread with butter   D. meat or fish with vegetables

( ) 5. Rose answered the letter _____.

    A. on New Year's Day   B. at the Lantern Festival

    C. on New Year's Eve   D. on Christmas Day

3

Films in Grand Movie Theatre This Week	
***HARRY POTTER*（Ⅲ）** American film Director: Alfonso Cuaron Stars: Daniel Radcliffe, Rupert Grint, Emma Waston Time: From Monday to Wednesday, at 6:00 pm Ticket price: $4.5	***KUNGFU HUSTLE*** Chinese Hong Kong film Director: Zhou Xingchi Stars: Zhou Xingchi, Yuan Hua, Liang Xiaolong Time: From Wednesday to Friday, at 9:00 pm. Ticket price: $5
A WORLD WITHOUT THIEVES Chinese film Director: Feng Xiaogang Stars: Liu Dehua, Liu Ruoying, Ge You, Li Bingbing Time: From Friday to Sunday, at 6:30 pm Ticket price: $6 (half on Sunday for children)	***TROY*** American film Director: Wolfgang Petersen Stars: Julian Glover, Brian Cox, Nathan Jones, Adoni Maropis Time: From Tuesday to Saturday, at 9:30 pm Ticket price: $5.5

Choose the right answer:

( ) 1. There will be _____ in Grand Movie Theatre this week.

    A. one Chinese film   B. two Chinese films

    C. three American films   D. a lot of foreign films

( ) 2. If a man with his child goes to Grand Movie Theatre on Sunday, they will pay

_____ for the film.

    A. $12   B. $9   C. $6   D. $5

(   ) 3. If you are free on Sunday evening, you can see the film _____ in Grand Movie Theatre.

    A. *Kung fu Hustle*   B. *A World Without Thieves*

    C. *Troy*   D. *Harry Potter*(Ⅲ)

(   ) 4. You can see three films either on _____ or on _____.

    A. Wednesday; Friday   B. Tuesday; Wednesday

    C. Thursday; Friday   D. Saturday; Sunday

(   ) 5. From the poster, we know _____ is a director and actor in the film.

    A. Alfonso Cuaron   B. Feng Xiaogang

    C. Wolfgang Petersen   D. Zhou Xingchi

4

The first stage	The second stage	The third stage
Time：October 15th, 2003 Spaceship：Shenzhou Ⅴ Main events： Chinese spaceman Yang Liwei was sent up into space. He went around the earth 14 times in his one-day flight. China became the third country to succeed in manned space flight.	Time：October 12th, 2005 Spaceship：Shenzhou Ⅵ Main events： Chinese spacemen Fei Junlong and Nie Haisheng were both sent up into space. On October 17th, the two Chinese space heroes safely returned to the earth.	Future plans： 1. China will make a manned moon landing at a proper(适当的) time around 2017. 2. China plans to set up a permanent(永久的) spacelab. and build its engineering system in the near future.

Choose the right answer：

(   ) 1. The Chinese spaceman travelling in space in the autumn of 2003 is _____.

    A. Yang Liwei   B. Fei Junlong   C. Nie Haisheng   D. Zhang Zhigang

(   ) 2. Before China, how many countries had already sent their spacemen into space?

    A. Only one.   B. Two.   C. Three.   D. We don't know.

(   ) 3. Shenzhou Ⅴ circled the earth in space _____.

    A. once   B. four times   C. five times   D. fourteen times

(   ) 4. During the second stage, the Chinese spacemen stayed in space for _____.

    A. one day   B. four days   C. five days   D. fourteen days

( ) 5. Chinese spacemen will possibly walk on the moon around _____.

    A. 2008   B. 2009   C. 2010   D. 2017

5

We can find ads everywhere. Here are some ads. Please read them carefully.

---

① SUMMER JOB

Are you easy-going and outgoing? Do you like writing and talking with people? Do you like writing stories? If you want to work for our newspaper as a reporter, please call Owen on 88045288.

Working hours: 2:00 pm~11:30 pm every day

---

② A WOMAN TEACHER WANTED

Are you good at drawing, dancing or singing? Do you like playing with children? If your answer is "Yes", then we have a job for you as an art teacher.

Working hours: 9:00 am~4:30 pm from Monday to Friday

Age: From 20 to 36

Salary: ￥2 000 per month

Tel: 025 - 58894528

Fax: 025 - 58894528

---

③ COOK WANTED

Are you hard-working? Do you like to serve for people? Can you cook delicious food? If your answer is "Yes", then you can get a good job in our restaurant as a cook.

Our restaurant is on Shanxi Road.

Salary: ￥1 500 per month

Tel: 025 - 45239958

---

④ CLEANER WANTED

Are you good at doing housework? Can you make a large house clean and tidy? If you hope to get the job paid at ￥20 an hour, call us between 8:00 and 11:30 tomorrow morning.

Tel: 83428000

Choose the right answer:

( ) 1. The above job advertisements are maybe from _____.

A. a newspaper   B. a story book
C. a science book   D. a guide book

(   ) 2. If a cleaner cleans a house for three hours at a time, twice a week, how much money will the cleaner get in a month?

A. ￥480.   B. ￥60.   C. ￥120.   D. ￥360.

(   ) 3. Can Mrs Brown, a 38-year-old woman teacher, get the job as an art teacher in the school?

A. Yes, she can.   B. No, she can't.
C. Probably she can.   D. We don't know.

(   ) 4. If you are interested in cooking delicious food, you can call somebody on _____ for a job.

A. 83428000   B. 45239958   C. 58894528   D. 88045288

(   ) 5. If you enjoy writing and want to have a job during your summer holiday, you will be interested in the job in _____.

A. ad ①   B. ad ②   C. ad ③   D. ad ④

6

Working people in Hong Kong are always busy in the daytime. They don't have enough time to enjoy themselves. If you are one of those people, come and join us! We'll take a night-time cruise(乘船游览) around the Victoria Harbour(维多利亚港). You can see fantastic city lights during the trip, and you can also enjoy a wonderful dinner on the junk(帆船) if you like.

Harbour Night Cruise

Time: 6:30 pm~10:00 pm(Monday~Friday)

　　　7:30 pm~12:00 pm(Saturday&Sunday)

Price: 　　　　　　　an adult　　　a child under 12

　(With dinner)　　300 yuan　　200 yuan

　(Without dinner)　220 yuan　　140 yuan

Ticket office: Harbour Travel Service (No. 30 Lam Ming Street)

Place to start: Star Company (No. 98 Cyberport Road)

Choose the right answer:

(   ) 1. What transport will people use during the trip?

A. They'll take a train.   B. They'll take the underground.
C. They'll take a junk.   D. They'll take a plane.

(   ) 2. Today is Friday. How long can people enjoy the night cruise tomorrow?

A. Three hours.   B. Three and a half hours.

C. Four hours.　　　　　　　　D. Four and a half hours.

(　) 3. People can enjoy the _____ during the cruise.

A. cool wind　　　　　　　　B. city lights

C. tall buildings　　　　　　　D. wonderful bridges

(　) 4. You will go to _____ to buy tickets.

A. Star Company　　　　　　　B. No. 30 Cyberport Road

C. Harbour Travel Service　　　D. No. 98 Lam Ming Street

(　) 5. Mr and Mrs Thomas with their 8-year-old son want to take the trip. How much can they save if they don't have dinner on the junk?

A. 220 yuan.　　　　　　　　B. 200 yuan.

C. 140 yuan.　　　　　　　　D. 300 yuan.

7

Dates	Huaihai	Yipinmei
	Prices (3 nights)	Prices (3 nights)
1 Jan. ～31 Mar.	￥480	￥570
1 Apr～30 Apr. (closed)	—	—
1 May～31 May	￥600	￥780
1 Jun～31 Sept.	￥750	￥840
1 Oct. ～31 Dec.	￥540	￥630

Choose the right answer:

(　) 1. Yipinmei Hotel is _____ than Huaihai Hotel.

A. cheaper　　　B. bigger　　　C. cleaner　　　D. dearer

(　) 2. I want to stay in the Yipinmei Hotel for five Hights in August. I need _____.

A. ￥1 400　　　B. ￥1 200　　　C. ￥1 000　　　D. ￥800

(　) 3. The two hotels are open for _____ months of the year.

A. nine　　　B. ten　　　C. eleven　　　D. twelve

(　) 4. It is cheaper to stay in Huaihai Hotel in May than it is in _____.

A. November　　　B. August　　　C. March　　　D. October

(　) 5. From October to December it is dearer to stay in Yipinmei Hotel than from _____ to _____.

A. June; August　　　　　　　B. May; July

C. July; September　　　　　　D. January; March

8

The following is Fred's schedule of this week. Read it carefully.

Monday	Go to see Millie in the Children's Hospital 3:00 pm~5:00 pm
Tuesday	Dancing class 8:30 am~10:30 am
Wednesday	Part-time job 12:00 am~6:00 pm
Thursday	See Dr Brown 10:30 am~11:30 am Part-time job 12:00 am~5:00 pm
Friday	Go to the station to meet Ann 9:00 am
Saturday	Meet Tom to study for test 2:00 pm~4:00 pm
Sunday	Birthday party for Kay 5:00 pm~8:00 pm

Choose the right answer:

(　　) 1. Where does Fred meet Ann?

A. At Brown's house.　　　　　B. In the hospital.

C. At the station.　　　　　D. At Kay's house.

(　　) 2. For how many hours a week does Fred do his part-time job?

A. Five hours.　　　　　B. Six hours.

C. Ten hours.　　　　　D. Eleven hours.

(　　) 3. ＿＿＿＿＿ is ill in hospital.

A. Brown　　　B. Millie　　　C. Tom　　　D. Kay

(　　) 4. Kay's birthday is on ＿＿＿＿＿.

A. Tuesday　　　B. Friday　　　C. Sunday　　　D. Thursday

(　　) 5. What does Fred do on Saturday afternoon?

A. Play football.　　　　　B. Study with Tom.

C. Have a dancing class.　　　　　D. Do part-time job.

9

Dear Isabelle,

If you look at a map of my country, you will find English name like Windsor,

French name like Quebec or Indian name like Manitoba. Strange, isn't it? Let me tell you more about my country. The history of my country is longer than that of the United States. A Viking(斯堪的纳维亚人), Leif Erickson, discovered Canada in 986. That was a long time before Christopher Columbus(哥伦布) discovered America in 1492.

Frenchmen Jacques Cartier and Champlain were the first explorers to come here, and that is why they called the country New France. But there were more English people than French people in Canada and it became English colony(殖民地) in 1763. After many wars Canada became independent in 1867. Now only about six million of us speak French. The area of Canada is about ten million square kilometres, and that is eighteen times as big as France and forty times as big as the UK, but only thirty million people live in Canada now. If you look at a map, you can see Canada is near Alaska. It is very cold in winter and very hot in summer. So, if you go to America one day, don't forget to visit Canada.

Love from your friend,
Rose

Choose the right answer:

( ) 1. Where does Rose live?
    A. In India.   B. In England.
    C. In Canada.   D. In France.

( ) 2. Who discovered Canada?
    A. Champlain.   B. Christopher Columbus.
    C. Jacques Cartier.   D. Leif Erickson.

( ) 3. This country is _____.
    A. as big as France   B. bigger than France
    C. smaller than France   D. the biggest in the world

( ) 4. How many people live in Canada now?
    A. Thirty million.   B. Six million.
    C. Ten million.   D. Forty million.

( ) 5. When did this country become independent?
    A. In 1492.   B. In 1867.   C. In 1944.   D. In 986.

10

---

① HOUSE TO RENT

Older house to rent in city centre. One bedroom and one kitchen. Near an important station. Buses pass back door.

$475/month Phone: 352 - 0178

---

② WELCOME TO OUR DANCE CLUB
Free lessons. Every Saturday evening. Bring your favourite CDs. Call Bridge at: 520 - 1928

③ SWIMMING LESSONS FOR STUDENTS
Newquay Training Centre July 8～10

④ WORK WANTED
Strong boys pleased to work in gardens or do housework. 3 hours a week. See Tom.

Choose the right answer:

Look at ad ①

Susan is looking for a house to rent. It doesn't matter how old and how expensive it is. She has got to study for her exams, so the house must be quiet.

(　　) 1. Susan doesn't want to rent the house in the ad because _____.

      A. it's too cold   B. it's too expensive

      C. there is only one bedroom   D. it's too noisy

Look at ad ②

Mum: Look at that ad for the Dance Club! The lessons are free. You can join it!

Daughter: You haven't read it carefully. On Saturday, I have an English lesson in the morning, an Art lesson in the afternoon and a Maths lesson in the evening. I want some free time!

(　　) 2. Why can't the daughter join the dance club?

      A. She has no CDs.   B. She has an Art lesson.

      C. She has an English lesson.   D. She has a Maths lesson.

Look at ad ③

Mr Klip's children are going to learn swimming. They'll have a holiday from July 1st to July 14th.

(　　) 3. How long will it take the children to learn to swim in the centre?

      A. 3 days.   B. 4 days.   C. 1 week.   D. 2 weeks.

Look at ad ④

Nick wants to work in a garden. He thinks it's an exciting place. It's hard work, but he can do it.

(　　) 4. What does Nick need to do if he chooses to do the garden work?

      A. To help Tom with his lesson.

B. To look after Tom.

C. To look after the flowers and grass.

D. To do the washing for 3 hours a week.

(　　) 5. How many phone numbers do the ads give us?

A. One. 　　B. Two. 　　C. Three. 　　D. Four.

11

Come and see the Indian elephants and the new tigers from northeast of China. The beautiful birds from England are ready to sing songs for you, and the monkeys from Mount Emei will be happy to talk to you. The lovely dogs from Australia want to laugh at you. Sichuan pandas will play balls for you. The giraffes from Africa are waiting to look down on you.

Tickets：　　　　　　　　　　Opening time：

Grown-ups：￥3　　　　　　　9 am～4 pm(Monday～Thursday

Children：Over 1. 4 m ￥2　　　10 am～3 pm(Friday～Sunday)

　　　　　Under 1. 4 m Free

Keep the zoo clean!

Do not touch, give food or go near to the animals.

Choose the right answer：

(　　) 1. Why does the writer introduce so many animals from different places to us?

A. To frighten us in the zoo.

B. To make us lovely in the zoo.

C. To attract us to the zoo.

D. To show animals can do everything.

(　　) 2. How much does Mr Smith have to pay if he visits the zoo with his son of three?

A. ￥3. 　　B. ￥4. 　　C. ￥5. 　　D. ￥6.

(　　) 3. At which of the following time can we visit the zoo?

A. At 8：30 am Wednesday. 　　B. At 9：30 am Friday.

C. At 2 pm Sunday. 　　D. At 5 pm Tuesday.

(　　) 4. A：What should we do in the zoo?

B：We should _____.

A. spit everywhere 　　B. throw things everywhere

C. keep the zoo clean 　　D. keep the zoo full

(　　) 5. From the passage we can infer(推断) a giraffe must be a very _____ animal.

| A. fat | B. short | C. strong | D. tall |

12

	Monday	Tuesday	Wednesday	Thursday	Friday
8:00~8:45	Maths	Chinese	English	Maths	Chinese
8:55~9:40	English	Maths	Chinese	Chinese	Computer
10:00~10:45	Art	Physics	Biology	Politics	Computer
10:55~11:40	PE	English	Maths	Chemistry	English
1:00~1:45	History	Geography	Physics	History	Maths
2:00~2:45	Music	Chemistry	PE	English	Biology
2:55~3:40	Chinese	Class Meeting	Politics	Chinese	Geography

Choose the right answer:

( ) 1. They have an Art class on _____.

A. Monday   B. Tuesday   C. Wednesday   D. Thursday

( ) 2. They have _____ Chinese classes every week.

A. 3   B. 4   C. 5   D. 6

( ) 3. A: How long will they rest for lunch break?

B: For _____.

A. 60 minutes   B. 70 minutes   C. 80 minutes   D. 90 minutes

( ) 4. They have _____ classes only on Monday and Wednesday.

A. Art   B. Music   C. Biology   D. PE

( ) 5. They can send and get e-mails from _____ to _____ in Computer classes on Friday.

A. 8:00; 9:40   B. 8:55; 10:45

C. 10:00; 11:40   D. 2:00; 3:40

13

The following is a menu of Jordan Bar.

Breakfast (from 7:30 to 10:30)

Orange, tomato, apple juice ·· $0.75

Grapefruit half ·· $0.65

Bananas ·· $0.75

1 egg，toast and coffee	……………………………	$1.25
2 eggs，toast and coffee	……………………………	$1.50
Boiled or fried eggs with bacon	……………………	$2.95
Boiled or fried eggs	……………………………	$2.00
Coffee	……………………………………	$0.35
Tea	………………………………………	$0.25
Hot chocolate	…………………………………	$0.30
Milk	………………………………………	$0.20

Choose the right answer：

(　) 1. What can't you have in Jordan Bar?

      A. Tea.　　　　B. Milk.　　　　C. Beer.　　　　D. Eggs.

(　) 2. When can you have breakfast in the bar?

      A. At 6：30 am　　　　　　B. At 8：00 am

      C. At 11：00 am　　　　　　D. At 7：00 am

(　) 3. How much is a glass of tomato juice?

      A. $0.25.　　B. $0.65.　　C. $0.75.　　D. $1.50.

(　) 4. What is the price of a cup of hot chocolate?

      A. $0.20.　　B. $0.30.　　C. $1.30.　　D. $0.25.

(　) 5. Tommy always has his breakfast here. He has a glass of apple juice, a fried

      egg with bacon and a cup of coffee. How much is this breakfast?

      A. $4.05.　　B. $3.95.　　C. $4.20.　　D. $3.50.

14

Are you interested in the following courses? Please read them and make a decision.

Name	Understanding Computers	Stopping Smoking	Typing
About The Course	This course is for people who do not know very much about computers but need to learn about them. You will learn what computers are, what they can and can not do, and how to use them.	Did you try to stop smoking but failed? Now it is time to do it using the latest methods. This twelve-hour course will help you do it.	This course is for those who want to learn to type, as well as those who want to make their typing better. You are tested in the first class and begin practising at one of eight different skill levels. This allows you to learn at your own speed.
Money	Course：$75 Equipment：$10	Course：$30	Course：$125 Material：$25

续　表

Name	Understanding Computers	Stopping Smoking	Typing
Time	Jan. 7, 14, 21, 28 Saturday 9:00 am~12:00 am	Jul. 4, 11, 18, 25 Monday 4:00 pm~7:00 pm	2 hours each evening for 2 weeks. New classes begin every 2 weeks.
Teachers	Joseph Smith, an experienced professor in the computer <u>field</u>.	Dr John Goode, a practising psychologist(心理学家).	A number of best business education teachers who have successfully taught typing courses before.

Choose the right answer:

(　　) 1. How much does the computer course cost?

A. $85.　　　　B. $65.　　　　C. $125.　　　　D. $75.

(　　) 2. How many hours does the whole computer course last?

A. 3.　　　　　　　　　　B. 9:00 am~12:00 am.

C. 28.　　　　　　　　　　D. 12.

(　　) 3. All the students taking the Typing course _____.

A. are beginners　　　　　B. are tested when they finish the course

C. work at their own speed　D. must go through all the eight levels

(　　) 4. The underlined word "field" means _____ in Chinese in the passage.

A. 田野　　　　　B. 方面　　　　　C. 领域　　　　　D. 专业

(　　) 5. Which of the following is right?

A. The Understanding Computers course begins on July 4.

B. The Understanding Computers course is on every Saturday evening in January.

C. The Stopping Smoking course is on Monday afternoon in January.

D. The Typing course will cost you $150.

15

Channel	Time	Name of program	Type of program
ATV	7:00	*News*	News
	8:30	*Good Friend Contest*	Game Show
	9:20	*Chinese Mothers*	Documentary Special
	12:00	*Tokyo Love Story*	Soap Opera

Channel	Time	Name of program	Type of program
BTV	7:40	*China Sports*	Sports Show
	9:20	*Happy Family*	Drama
	11:00	*Face to Face*	Talk Show
CTV	9:30	*China Music*	Music
	13:40	*Romantic Dream*	Fashion Show
	22:00	*CTV Football Magazine*	Sports Show

Choose the right answer：

( ) 1. What time does the program *Chinese Mothers* begin?

A. 10:00.   B. 9:20.   C. 13:30.   D. 22:00.

( ) 2. What type is the program *Tokyo Love Story*?

A. Sitcom.   B. Sports Show.   C. Soap Opera.   D. Music.

( ) 3. Which two programs begin at the same time?

A. *Face to Face* and *Romantic Dream*.

B. *Happy Family* and *China Music*.

C. *Chinese Mothers* and *CTV Football Magazine*.

D. *Chinese Mothers* and *Happy Family*.

( ) 4. Which program is Fashion Show?

A. *Romantic Dream*.   B. *News*.

C. *Face to Face*.   D. *China Sports*.

( ) 5. Which channel has the program *Good Friend Contest*?

A. ATV.   B. BTV.   C. CTV.   D. CCTV.

16

Cable TV	City TV
6:30 pm *Today's China：Guangzhou*	6:10 pm *Cartoon City*
7:00 pm *News*	7:05 pm *World Cities：Sydney*
7:30 pm *Weather Report*	8:10 pm *Agriculture*
7:40 pm *Today's Focus*	9:00 pm *The Story of Earth*
8:00 pm *TV Play：Red Beans*	10:05 pm *Economy 30 Minutes*

Cable TV	City TV
10:00 pm *World News*	10:45 pm *News in English*
10:30 pm *Sports Report*	11:15 pm *Fashion Show*
11:00 pm *On the Screen Tomorrow*	12:00 pm *On the Screen Tomorrow*

Choose the right answer：

（　）1. If your Australian friend doesn't know Chinese, you can tell him to watch _____.
　　　　A. Cable TV at 7:00 pm　　　　　B. Cable TV at 10:00 pm
　　　　C. City TV at 10:05 pm　　　　　D. City TV at 10:45 pm

（　）2. If you want to know more about Guangzhou, which programme will you choose?
　　　　A. *Today's China*.　　　　　B. *World Cities*.
　　　　C. *Today's Focus*.　　　　　D. *The Story of Earth*.

（　）3. If you are interested in the latest fashion, you may watch *Fashion Show* at _____.
　　　　A. 10:00 pm　　B. 7:00 pm　　C. 8:10 pm　　D. 11:15 pm

（　）4. Most children love watching _____.
　　　　A. *Weather Report*　　　　　B. *Cartoon City*
　　　　C. *Economy 30 Minutes*　　　D. *Red Beans*

（　）5. Which of the following is true?
　　　　A. Cable TV can tell us some knowledge about farming.
　　　　B. *On the Screen Tomorrow* tells you tomorrow's programmes.
　　　　C. *Today's Focus* is about the story of Earth.
　　　　D. *Weather Report* is on City TV.

17

　　Li Ping is a Grade Eight student in Nanjing Sunshine Secondary School. The table below is his mid-term self-assessment(自我评价). He draws faces to show his progress：

Excellent　　　　　OK　　　　　Weak

Read the table and find out how well Li Ping is doing.

Item \ Unit	Unit 1 Past and Present	Unit 2 Travelling	Unit 3 Online travel
Vocabulary	Opposites 😐	Suffixes 'ful' and 'less' 🙂	Words about computers 😐
Grammar	Present prefect tense 🙁	Past continuous tense 😐	Passive voice 🙁
Study skills/Pronunciation	Using a dictionary 🙂	Linking words 😐	Organizing information 😐
Main task	A report 😐	My best holiday 🙂	Favourite educational computer game 🙁

Choose the right answer：

(　) 1. Li Ping thinks he did best in _____ in Unit 1.

　　A. opposites 　　　　　　　B. using a dictionary

　　C. a report 　　　　　　　D. present perfect tense

(　) 2. What does Li Ping need to improve in Unit 1?

　　A. Present perfect tense. 　　B. Using a dictionary.

　　C. A report. 　　　　　　　D. Opposites.

(　) 3. Which do you think Li Ping does well in?

　　A. Present perfect tense.

　　B. Passive voice.

　　C. Organizing information.

　　D. Favourite educational computer game.

(　) 4. What is Li Ping NOT very good at in Unit 2?

　　A. Suffixes "ful"and "less". 　　B. Past continuous tense.

　　C. Linking words. 　　　　　　D. My best holiday.

(　) 5. From the table we know Li Ping is weak in _____.

　　A. Vocabulary 　　　　　　　B. Main task

　　C. Study skills/Pronunciation 　　D. Grammar

18

Welcome to Franklin Hotel. To make your stay as enjoyable as possible，we hope you will use our facilities(设施) to the full.

Dining Room：Breakfast is severed in the dinning room from 8 am to 9：00 am. Also the room staff(服务员) may bring breakfast to your room at any time after 7 am. If this happens，please fill out a card and hang outside your door when you go to bed. Lunch is from 12 am to 2：30 pm. Dinner is from 7：30 pm to 9 pm.

Room Service：This operates 24 hours a day；phone the reception desk，and your message will be passed on to the staff.

Telephones：To make a telephone call，dial（拨）0 for Reception and ask to be connected. We apologize for delays if the lines are very busy. There are also public telephones in the entrance hall near the Reception desk. Tell Reception if early calls are needed.

Shop：The hotel shop is open for presents，gifts and goods from 9 am to 5：30 pm.

Laundry：We have a laundry in the building，and will wash，iron and return your clothes within 24 hours. Ask the room staff to collect them.

Bar：The hotel bar is open from 12 am to 2 pm and 7 pm to 1 am.

Banking：The Reception staff will cash cheques and exchange any foreign money for you.

Choose the right answer：

（　） 1. You would see this notice _____.

　　A. in a hotel bar

　　B. in a hotel dining room

　　C. in a bedroom of a large international hotel

　　D. at the entrance of a small family hotel

（　） 2. You have arrived at the hotel at 2 am and want a quick meal. What should you do?

　　A. Go to the hotel shop.

　　B. Go to the hotel bar.

　　C. Hang a message outside your door.

　　D. Phone reception desk.

（　） 3. You have come back to the hotel just to make an urgent（紧急） phone call. But you notice a lot of people around the Reception desk. Judging from the notice，it would be the quickest to _____.

　　A. go to your room and phone from there

　　B. use one of the public telephones in the entrance hall

　　C. ask at the Reception desk

　　D. go out again and look for a public phone box

（　） 4. The underlined word "laundry" in the above passage means" _____ ".

　　A. tailor's shop　　B. operating room　　C. clothes shop　　D. washhouse

(　) 5. The passage tells us that _____.

    A. the hotel offers at least seven kinds of service

    B. it's not convenient（方便）to stay up in the hotel

    C. you'll have the trouble without the money of the country the hotel belongs to

    D. you can shop at any time inside the hotel

19

    Peter King and Mary King are brother and sister. Peter King is 15 while Mary King is 13. One day they went to see a doctor. Peter had a bad cold, so the doctor gave him some pills to take. Mary had a bad cough, so the doctor gave her some cough medicine.

    These are the words on the bottle of medicine:

        Shake well before use.

        Take three times daily after meals.

        Dose: Adults — 2 teaspoonfuls.

        Children 8~10 — 1 teaspoonful.

        Children 4~7 — 1/2 teaspoonful.

        Not suitable for children below the age of 4.

        Store in a cold place.

        Use before October 2003.

Choose the right answer:

(　) 1. The medicine is suitable for _____.

    A. children   B. adults

    C. both children and adults   D. only small babies

(　) 2. When you take the medicine, you should _____.

    A. have the meal first   B. shake it fully

    C. have the meal later   D. Both A and B

(　) 3. Mary should take _____ a day.

    A. 1/2 teaspoonful   B. 2 teaspoonfuls

    C. 3 teaspoonfuls   D. 6 teaspoonfuls

(　) 4. If Peter had a cough, he would take the amount for _____.

    A. children   B. adults

    C. babies   D. youth

(　) 5. If Mary had a bad cough one week before Christmas in 2003, she may _____.

    A. have a rest at home   B. lie in bed for a week

    C. take this medicine left   D. go to see a doctor again

20

When prices are low, people will buy more, and when prices are high, they will buy less. Every shopper knows this. But at the same time, producers want higher prices for their goods when they make more goods. According to the economic point of view, changes in the prices of goods cause changes in supply and demand(供求). As is shown in the graph, people buy fewer shoes as the price of shoes goes up. On the contrary, a decrease(the opposite word of increase) in the price causes an increase in demand.

The Number of Shoes Sold

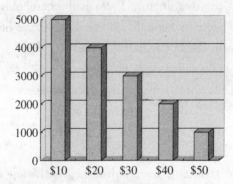

Business companies look for the perfect price at which the largest profit(利润) can be made. If the price of the shoes goes up to $50, people will not buy all of 3 000 shoes. The producers will have a surplus(剩余) of 2 000 shoes and they can only get $50 000. If the price of the shoes is lowered to $10, as many as 5 000 shoes can be sold. Still, only $50 000 is made.

Choose the right answer:

(　　) 1. The main idea of the first paragraph is that _____.

　　A. the lower the price is, the fewer people will buy it.

　　B. producers want to make more money by making fewer goods

　　C. every shopkeeper knows the price of goods

　　D. changes in the prices of goods may affect both supply and demand

(　　) 2. We can learn from the graph that if the price of the shoes is lowered down to $20, _____ shoes will be sold.

　　A. 2 000　　　　B. 3 000　　　　C. 4 000　　　　D. 5 000

(　　) 3. According to the graph, when shoe producers charge the shoes _____ for each, they will make most money.

　　A. $10　　　　B. $20　　　　C. $30　　　　D. $40

(　　) 4. What does the underlined word "graph" mean in Chinese?

　　A. 图表　　　　B. 图案　　　　C. 图画　　　　D. 图形

(　) 5. The text is mainly about _____.

  A. the perfect price for shoe producers

  B. how a graph could help us understand economic

  C. the relationship between supply and demand

  D. how prices affect supply and demand

 说明类

范文解析

When you are reading something in English, you may often come across a new word. What's the best way to know it?

You may look it up in the English-Chinese dictionary. It will tell you a lot about the word: the pronunciation, the part of speech(词性), the Chinese meaning and also how to use this word. But how can you know where the word is in thousands of English words? How to find it in the dictionary both quickly and correctly?

First, all the English words are arranged in the alphabetical order. In the dictionary you can first see the words beginning with the letter A, then B, C, D, E... That means if there are two words "desert" and "pull", "desert" will be certainly before "pull". Then if there are two words both beginning with the same letter, you may look at the second letter. Then the third, the fourth... For example, "pardon" is before "plough", "judge" before "just", etc.

Do you understand how to look up a word in a dictionary?

The dictionary will be your good friend. I hope you'll use it as often as possible in your English learning.

Choose the right answer:

(　) 1. When you don't know a word, the best way is _____.

  A. to ask your teacher   B. to think hard

  C. to give up   D. to look it up in a dictionary

(　) 2. When you look up a word in the English-Chinese dictionary, you should understand not only its Chinese meaning, but also _____.

  A. its pronunciation

  B. its part of speech

  C. the use of it

  D. its prunuciation, the part of speech and the use of it

(　) 3. In the English-Chinese dictionary, the first part is _____.

  A. the words beginning with the letter A

B. the words beginning with the letter E

C. the simple words

D. the very short words

(   ) 4. Here are four words："blind"，"murder"，"monument" and "boyhood".
   Their right order in the English-Chinese dictionary is _____.

  A. blind，boyhood，murder，monument

  B. blind，boyhood，monument，murder

  C. boyhood，blind，monument，murder

  D. monument，murder，blind，boyhood

(   ) 5. The English-Chinese dictionary is _____.

  A. useful in learning Chinese

  B. our good friend in learning Chinese

  C. our good friend in learning English

  D. not useful in learning English

【答案与解析】

1. **D** 可由文章第一段以及第二段第一句"When you are reading something in English, you may often come across a new word. What's the best way to know it?" "You may look it up in the English-Chinese dictionary."得知，当阅读英语遇到生词时，最好的方法就是查阅字典。因此本题答案明显是 D。

2. **D** 可由文章第二段中"It will tell you a lot about the word：the pronunciation, the part of speech(词性)，the Chinese meaning and also how to use this word."得知，在字典中查阅生词时，可以了解到一个生词的读音、词性、中文意思以及如何使用该词。而本题题干中提到，除了中文意思外，对于一个生词还需要了解哪些？那么应当是读音、词性和用法这三项，因此答案应当为 D。

3. **A** 文章第三段中提到"First, all the English words are arranged in the alphabetical order. In the dictionary you can first see the words beginning with the letter A, then B, C, D, E..."由此可知，在字典中首先看到的应当是以字母 A 开头的单词。因此答案显然为 A。

4. **B** 此题要注意正确运用字母排序法来进行排列。文章中提到"First, all the English words are arranged in the alphabetical order. In the dictionary you can first see the words beginning with the letter A, then B, C, D, E...". 此外还提到"Then if there are two words both beginning with the same letter, you may look at the second letter. Then the third, the fourth..."根据这个原则，在排列本题中的四个单词时，先看第一个字母可知，blind 和 boyhood 这两个词肯定在 monument 和 murder 之前，首先可排除 D 选项。接下来，再看第二个字母可知，blind 应在 boyhood 之前，而 monument 应在 murder 之前，由此可知正确顺序应为 B 选项。

5. **C** 这可由文章最后一段"The dictionary will be your good friend. I hope you'll

use it as often as possible in your English learning."得知,在学习英语的过程中,字典可以成为你的好朋友。因此答案应为 C。注意不要错选成 A 或 B 选项,因为整篇文章都是在讨论学习英语时可以利用字典,并没有提到学习中文的问题,所以 A,B 两项都与文章内容无关。而 D 选项又和文章所表达的意思正好相反,因此也是错误的。

实战演练

1

A good way to pass an exam is to work hard every day. You may not pass an exam if you don't work hard for most time and then work hard only a few days before the exam.

If you are taking an English exam, do not only learn rules of grammar. Try to read stories in English and speak English whenever you can.

Before you start the exam, read carefully over the question paper. Try to understand the exact meaning of each question before you pick up your pen to write. When you have at last finished your exam, read over your answer. Correct the mistakes if there are any and make sure that you have not missed anything out.

Choose the right answer:

( ) 1. How can you do well in an exam?

    A. Work hard every day.

    B. Be careful in doing the questions.

    C. Read over your answer before you hand in your paper.

    D. All of the above.

( ) 2. Learning rules of grammar _____ to pass an English exam.

    A. is enough   B. is not enough

    C. is not necessary   D. is of no use

( ) 3. It is NOT a good way _____.

    A. to read English stories

    B. to learn rules of grammar

    C. to speak English as much as possible

    D. to work hard only a few days before the exam

( ) 4. The underlined word "whenever" means _____.

    A. every time   B. what time

    C. at any time   D. forever

( ) 5. The underlined phrase "miss...out" means _____.

    A. think hard   B. not have enough time to do

C. not put in   D. give the wrong answer

2

The word you begin with is called a "base word". Let's use "happy" as our base word. Add the syllable "un-" before "happy" and you've made a new word, "unhappy". Can you tell how the meaning of "happy" was changed by reading the sentence below?

"Everybody was happy when the Blue Team won, and unhappy later when the Team lost."

By adding the syllable "un-" you added "not" to the meaning of the base word. The meaning, "happy" or "glad" was changed to "not happy" or "not glad".

A syllable that is added before a base word to change the meaning of the word is called a "prefix".

True or False：

(   ) 1. The word "unhappy" means "not happy".

(   ) 2. You can change the meaning of a word by adding a prefix.

(   ) 3. If you know the meaning of a prefix, you will easily guess the meaning of a new word.

(   ) 4. A prefix is a syllable that is added after a base word to change the meaning of the word.

(   ) 5. It is useful to learn prefixes.

3

You have already worked with prefixes and base words to make new words with added meanings. You can work with syllables at the ends of words, too.

A syllable that is added to the end of a word to add new meaning to the base word is called a "suffix".

Begin with the base word "speak" and add the suffix "-er" to make a new word "speaker". Can you tell the meaning that the suffix "-er" added to the meaning of the base word "speak" when you read the sentences below?

"Have you heard Dr Horn speak?"

"Yes, he's a good speaker."

"Speak" changes to "speaker" or "one who speaks". In the same way "listen" with the suffix "-er" added becomes "listener" or "one who listens".

True or False：

(   ) 1. A suffix is something added to the beginning of a word.

(   ) 2. "Speak" is a verb, and "speaker" is a noun.

(   ) 3. When you have a class meeting, the class teacher is often the speaker.

(　　) 4. If you are listening to the radio, you are a speaker.

(　　) 5. If you are listening to a tape, you are a listener.

4

Many people go to school for an education. They learn languages, history, politics, geography, physics, chemistry and mathematics. Others go to school to learn skills in order to make a living. School education is very important and useful. Yet, no one can learn everything from school. A teacher, no matter how much he knows, can not teach his students everything they want to know. The teacher's job is to show his students how to learn. He teaches them how to read and how to think. So, much more is to be learned outside school by the students themselves.

It is always more important to know how to study by oneself than to remember some facts or a formula(公式). It is actually quite easy to learn a certain fact in history or a formula in mathematics. But it is very difficult to use a formula in working out a maths problem. Great scientists before us didn't get everything from school. Their teachers only showed them the way. Edison didn't even finish primary school. But they were all so successful. Edison invented so many things for human beings. The reason for their success is that they know how to study. They read books that were not taught at school. They would ask many questions as they read. They did thousands of experiments. They worked hard all their lives, wasting not a single moment. Most important is that they know how to use their brains.

Choose the right answer:

(　　) 1. People go to school _____.

　　　　A. only to learn several subjects　　B. to make a living

　　　　C. to get an education　　　　　　D. only to learn skills

(　　) 2. According to the passage, what is the most important thing a teacher should do?

　　　　A. To teach his students everything he knows.

　　　　B. To know everything.

　　　　C. To teach the students how to think.

　　　　D. To teach the students how to study by themselves.

(　　) 3. To work out a maths problem, you need to know _____.

　　　　A. only a certain formula　　　　B. how to memorize some facts

　　　　C. only some facts　　　　　　　D. the method to solve it

(　　) 4. Why were many scientists so successful?

　　　　A. They received good education.

　　　　B. They were very clever.

C. They knew how to learn.

D. They learned lots of facts and formulas.

(　　) 5. How did great scientists study?

A. They read a lot of books and asked many questions while reading.

B. They did thousands of experiments.

C. They always worked hard and never wasted time.

D. All of the above.

5

All students need to have good study habits. When you have good study habits, you learn things quickly. You also remember them easily.

Do you like to study in the living room? This is not a good place, because it is usually too noisy. You need to study in a quiet place, like your bedroom. A quiet place will help you only to think about one thing.

When you study, do not think about other things at the same time. Only think about your homework. If you do this, you will do your homework more quickly, and you will make fewer mistakes.

Good study habits are very important. If you do not have them, try to learn them. If yours are already good, try to make them better.

Choose the right answer:

(　　) 1. How do you learn things when you have good study habits?

A. All students need to have good study habits.

B. We will learn things quickly.

C. Do not think about other things.

D. Only think about our homework.

(　　) 2. When do you remember things easily?

A. When we have good study habits.

B. When you study.

C. When you learn things.

D. When we need to have good study habits.

(　　) 3. What shouldn't you do at the same time when you study?

A. We should have good study habits.

B. We should learn things quickly.

C. We should remember things easily.

D. We should not think about other things.

(　　) 4. What must you only think about when you study?

A. We must only think about good study habits.

B. We must only think about other things.

C. We must only think about our homework.

D. We must only think about mistakes.

(　) 5. If you do not have good study habits, what must you do?

A. We must try to make them better.

B. We must try to learn them and have them.

C. We must try to make fewer mistakes.

D. We must try to do our homework quickly.

6

When you want to go shopping, decide how much money you can spend on new clothes. Think about the kind of clothes you really need. Then look for those clothes on sale.

There are labels inside all new clothes. The labels tell you how to take care of your clothes. The label on a shirt may tell you to wash it in warm water. The label on a sweater may tell you to wash it in cold water. The label on a coat may say "Dry-clean only. Washing may ruin this coat." If you do as the instructions on the labels, you can keep your clothes looking best. Many clothes today must be dry-cleaned. You will save money if you buy clothes that can be washed. You can save money if you buy clothes that are well made. Well-made clothes last longer. They look good even after they have been washed many times. Clothes that cost more money do not always fit better. Sometimes less expensive clothes look and fit better than more expensive clothes.

Choose the right answer:

(　) 1. Which of the following is NOT mentioned when we want to go shopping?

A. Think how much money we can spend on new clothes.

B. Think about the kind of clothes we really need.

C. Think how old we are.

D. Look for those clothes on sale.

(　) 2. There are labels _____ all new clothes.

A. inside 　　　B. behind 　　C. next to 　　　D. at

(　) 3. The labels tell us _____.

A. how to wear our clothes 　　B. how much the clothes cost

C. how to take care of our clothes 　D. how to sell the clothes

(　) 4. According to the passage, dry cleaning _____.

A. is impossible 　　　　B. can save our money

C. is not good for clothes 　　D. is expensive

(　) 5. If we buy well-made clothes, we can _____.

A. talk freely   B. make friends easily

C. save money   D. have more time

7

Getting along with a step-parent can be quite different from getting on with others. After all, when you meet a new person—such as a new friend—you get to introduce him or her into your life slowly, and you have time to think what he or she will do in your life and how you really feel about them. Step-parents can feel like strangers who suddenly come into your life.

Everyone's life is different. Some people find themselves with a new step-parent after a parent's death; others face the same problem after their parents' divorce. Some parents need years to meet and marry other people. Some remarry almost soon after the divorce. When a parent remarries, you may find yourself in a family with stepbrothers and stepsisters, or, after a few years, with much younger half-brothers or half-sisters.

There are no easy answers to how to accept a step-parent because of different situations. Someone can accept it easily. But someone can't. It may take him or her some time to accept the fact: the family is changing. Family members should be friendly to each other. In such a way, they can keep a nice family again.

True or False:

(　　) 1. Building a relationship with a step-parent is different from building other relationships.

(　　) 2. Some people may find a new step-parent come into their life suddenly.

(　　) 3. Most people can accept a step-parent easily.

(　　) 4. Some people need time to accept a step-parent and a new family.

(　　) 5. Being friendly to each other is most important for people to keep a nice family.

8

Body language shows all kinds of feelings and is sometimes more important than spoken language.

A smile is a usual facial expression—it shows that you are friendly to others. However, it does not always mean that you are happy. A smile can hide other feelings, like anger, fear or worry.

In most countries, nodding the head up and down shows agreement, while shaking the head means that you do not agree, or that you would not like to do something.

If you stand holding your arms across your chest, you may be protecting yourself—just from a conversation(谈话) you do not want! If you sit looking at the person you are talking to and then turn toward to him, it shows that you are interested. If you roll your eyes and turn your head away, most likely you do not believe what you are hearing, or you do not like what you hear.

Choose the right answer:

( ) 1. Body language shows _____.

    A. all kinds of feelings   B. some special feelings

    C. nothing   D. only happy feelings

( ) 2. When a person smiles, _____.

    A. it always shows he is very happy

    B. it always means he hides some feelings

    C. there may be some other feelings behind the smile

    D. it shows he is angry, worried or frightened

( ) 3. _____, nodding heads up and down shows he agrees with you.

    A. In most countries   B. In all countries

    C. In some countries   D. In Western countries

( ) 4. If a man stands holding his arms across his chest, it means _____.

    A. he wants to protect himself from a conversation he doesn't want

    B. he is very interested in the conversation

    C. he is pleased with the man he is talking to

    D. he wants to know more about the man he is talking to

( ) 5. If a person doesn't like what someone is saying, he may _____.

    A. listen carefully   B. roll his eyes and turn his head away

    C. sit looking at him/her   D. keep on talking to him/her

9

Some children may have behaviour(行为) problems in school, from talking in class to fighting in the playground. As a parent, what can you do? The following may help you.

Try to learn about your child's relationship with the teacher. Often when a child is having behaviour problems in school, it usually seems that the teacher doesn't like him or her. Often when your child has behaviour problems, he or she is just trying to get the teacher's attention. But if your child does something and that makes it difficult for the teacher to like him or her, move your child to a different classroom.

Sometimes going to a place where he or she is not succeeding(有成就感的) every day can push a child into behaviour problems. If you can, try having a day off from school to do something with your child and he or she really enjoys that. For example, you can spend the day at the beach, or just play in the backyard. Anyway just give your child a break.

If the child knows he or she is loved, that can make him or her out of a hard time. So you can sometimes give your child something special that he or she can put in the pocket, like a little note saying "I love you and you're great".

True or False:

(   ) 1. Fighting with other children is a kind of behaviour problem.

(   ) 2. When a child does something wrong, he or she may just want to get his or her teacher's attention.

(   ) 3. A child with behaviour problems should not go to school.

(   ) 4. Parents must put something in children's pockets to make them happy.

(   ) 5. Parents should let their children know they are loved.

10

No family is perfect. Even in the happiest home, things happen and parents disagree from time to time. Most children worry when their parents argue. Loud voices and angry words can make them feel afraid, sad, or upset. Even their not talking to each other can upset children.

What does it mean when parents argue? First, just like children, when parents get upset, they might cry, shout, or say things they don't really mean to. Sometimes an argument might not mean anything. Second, just like children, parents might argue more if they are not feeling well, if they have a lot of things to do for their work or if they have other worries.

OK, if your parents argue more often, you can talk to someone your family believe. They can help by telling your parents to listen to each other and talk about their problems without shouting. Though it may take some work and time, people in families can always learn to get along better. Being part of a family means everyone joins together to make life better for each other. With love and understanding, families can solve almost any problem.

True or False:

(   ) 1. Children will feel unhappy when their parents argue.

(   ) 2. When parents are angry with each other, they should not talk to each other.

(   ) 3. Parents may argue just because they are worried, sad or tired.

(   ) 4. If parents often argue, it may take some time for them to learn how to get along with each other.

(   ) 5. For a family to be happy, there should be love and understanding.

11

Teenagers' parents care about their children's studies more than anything else.

They can do everything for their children. Many of the parents spend most of their free time on their children's studies. Some parents even pay much money to find tutors for their children. It seems that receiving a better education or entering a key university is their only hope for children.

Of course, parents should pay attention to children's test scores. However, it also causes problems. Many children are too nervous. Some of them run away from home at times. So it's important to foster(培养) their abilities and personal qualities. Teachers and parents must teach them how to survive and how to be healthy in mind, body and spirit.

True or False:

(　　) 1. Teenagers' parents are willing to do everything for their children.

(　　) 2. Parents are free, so they spend most time on their children's studies.

(　　) 3. A tutor means someone who gives private lessons to one or more students.

(　　) 4. Some children run away from home because they don't have money to go to school.

(　　) 5. Teachers at school should only teach students how to study.

12

More than 16 percent of Chinese middle school students have emotional problems caused by stress of too many exams. They feel nervous and worried from time to time. They fear they can't reach their parents' expectations(期望). An unhappy family life can also lead to depression(抑郁). According to a study of 2 961 middle school students, students who have problems can be divided into two groups: students in their first and second years of secondary schools and those in their last year at high schools. The result also showed that emotional problems increase as students get older. The percentage of students with emotional problems in secondary schools is around 13 percent, while the number of students in high schools reaches about 19 percent.

Now more and more people have realized these problems. The Chinese experts say that youth organizations should create nice environment for the healthy growth of young people with the help of the whole society. Students should also be encouraged to take part in different kinds of social activities, such as serving the elderly, cleaning the parks, helping the homeless and planting trees... Through service, they can touch the lives of others and make their lives more colourful.

Choose the right answer:

(　　) 1. Over 16% students have emotional problems caused by _____.

　　　　A. their parents　　　　　　　B. too many exams

　　　　C. their friends　　　　　　　D. their unhappy families

(   ) 2. Some students fear _____ if they don't get good marks in exams.

       A. their parents will be disappointed

       B. they will lose their families

       C. their parents will suffer from depression

       D. their teachers will get angry with them

(   ) 3. Most students who have problems are in _____ different grades.

       A. two   B. three   C. four   D. five

(   ) 4. The study showed students in secondary schools _____ those in high schools.

       A. have fewer problems than   B. have more problems than

       C. have as many problems as   D. feel more stressed than

(   ) 5. Our society should offer the students _____.

       A. rich food   B. more money

       C. more parks   D. nice environment

13

Put an ice cube from your fridge into a glass of water. You have a piece of string (线) 10 centimetres long. The problem is to take out that piece of ice with the help of the string. But you must not touch the ice with your fingers.

You may ask your friends to try to do that when you are having dinner together. There is a salt-cellar on the table. You must use salt when you carry out this experiment.

First you put the string across the piece of ice. Then put some salt on the ice. Salt makes ice melt(融化). The ice round the string will begin to melt. But when it melts, it will lose heat. The cold ice cube will make the salt water freeze(结冰) again.

After a minute or two you may raise the piece of string and with it you will raise your piece of ice!

This experiment can be very useful to you. If, for example, there is ice near the door of your house, you must use very much salt to melt all the ice. If you don't put enough salt, the water will freeze again.

Choose the right answer:

(   ) 1. We must use _____ when we carry out this experiment.

       A. a fridge   B. some food   C. a table   D. some salt

(   ) 2. How long will it take to carry out this experiment?

       A. More than three minutes.   B. Five minutes or so.

       C. Only one minute or two.   D. About ten minutes.

(   ) 3. What is the task of this experiment?

A. Put the ice cube into the glass of water with the help of the string.

B. Take out the ice cube in the glass of water with the help of the string.

C. Take out the ice cube in the glass of water with your fingers.

D. Put some salt on the ice cube and then put the string across it.

(   ) 4. How many things at least are used in this experiment?

A. Three.   B. Four.   C. Six.   D. Seven.

(   ) 5. We can learn something about _____ from the passage.

A. physics   B. biology   C. chemistry   D. maths

14

Why do some people live to be 100 years old? If we study them, will we learn the ways of improving our health? There are some answers to these questions in an unusual place: the island of Okinawa(冲绳岛) in Japan.

Matsuko Suzuki, a Japanese gerontologist(老年医学专家), is an international expert on old age. Dr Suzuki is studying why Okinawa has more than double the Japanese average of centenarians(百岁老人). He has studied 521 centenarians from Okinawa. He says that if people eat a mainly vegetarian diet, they will live longer. He also says that if parents or grandparents live longer than average, their children will live longer too.

The centenarians on Okinawa are very active. They walk and they garden. If they have energy and strength, they help out with the farming work on this agricultural island. The pace of life is slower here than on the main island of Japan. People laugh about "Okinawa time." Dr Suzuki says that if people feel a lot of stress(压力), they will get sick more easily.

Dr Suzuki reports that old people do very well if they get respect and love. On Okinawa, everyone respects and values old people. Family life and religion(宗教) are very important. Dr Suzuki believes he will discover more reasons for longevity(长寿) if he continues with his study.

Choose the right answer:

(   ) 1. Which of the following is NOT the reason for longevity?

A. Living actively.   B. Helping with the farming work.

C. Lots of stress in life.   D. Good family life.

(   ) 2. What does "Okinawa time" mean in this passage?

A. Nice weather.   B. A harvest time.

C. The slow pace of life.   D. A busy life.

(   ) 3. We learn from the passage that people on Okinawa mainly live on _____.

A. farming   B. fishing

C. making machines D. receiving travelers

( ) 4. "People who laugh about Okinawa time" in the third paragraph refers to _____.

A. people on Okinawa B. people on the main island of Japan

C. people who study centenarians D. people of 100 years old

( ) 5. The passage does NOT SAY BUT IMPLIES(暗示) that _____.

A. less meat is one of the reasons for longevity

B. religion is not necessary for longevity

C. there are 521 centenarians on Okinawa

D. old people should live less actively

15

Do you feel a little sleepy after lunch? Well, that's normal. Your body naturally slows down then. What should you do about it? Don't reach for a coffee! Instead, take a nap.

There are many benefits of a daily nap. First of all, you are more efficient after napping. You remember things better and make fewer mistakes. Also, you can learn things more easily after taking a nap. A 20-minute nap can reduce information overload. It can also reduce stress. Finally, a nap may increase your self-confidence and make you more alert. It may even cheer you up.

But, there are some simple rules you should follow about taking a nap. First, take a nap in the middle of the day, about eight hours after you wake up. Otherwise, you may disturb your sleep-wake pattern. Next, a 20-minute nap is the best. If you sleep longer, you may fall into a deep sleep. After waking from a deep sleep, you will feel worse. Also, you should set an alarm clock. That means, you can fully relax during your nap. You won't have to keep looking at the clock so that you don't oversleep.

Now, the next time you feel sleepy after lunch, don't get stressed. Put your head down, close your eyes, and have forty winks.

Choose the right answer:

( ) 1. If you feel sleepy after lunch, you'd better _____.

A. slow down B. drink a cup of coffee

C. take a nap D. be more efficient

( ) 2. What is a good rule for taking a nap?

A. Use an alarm clock. B. Nap eight hours after waking up.

C. Sleep for about 20 minutes. D. All of the above.

( ) 3. According to the passage, what is NOT a benefit of napping?

A. It makes you stronger.

B. It makes you feel happier.

C. It gives you more self-confidence.

D. It improves your memory.

(　　) 4. Which may happen if an alarm clock is not used?

　　A. You may relax more.

　　B. You may feel too nervous to relax.

　　C. You may forget an important meeting.

　　D. You may not reduce your napping time.

(　　) 5. In the last paragraph, the underlined phrase "have forty winks" can be replaced by "_____".

　　A. do eye-protection exercises

　　B. close your eyes for forty times

　　C. have a short sleep during the daytime

　　D. pretend to have a quick nap after lunch

16

In Canada and United States, people enjoy entertaining(请客) at home. They often invite friends over for a meal, a party, or just for coffee and conversation.

Here are the kinds of things people say when they invite someone to their home:

"Would you like to come over for dinner Saturday night?"

"Hey, we're having a party on Friday. Can you come?"

To reply to an invitation, either say thank you and accept, or say you are sorry and give an excuse:

"Thanks, I'd love to. What time would you like me to come?" or "Oh, sorry. I've tickets for a movie."

Sometimes, however, people use expressions that should be like invitations but which are not real invitations. For example:

"Please come over for drink sometime."

"Why not get together for a party sometime?"

"Why don't you come over and see us sometime soon?"

They are really just polite ways of ending a conversation. They are not really invitations because they don't mention a specific(确定的) time or date. They just show that the person is trying to be friendly. To reply to expressions like these, people just say "Sure, that would be great!" or "OK. Yes, thanks."

So next time when you hear what sounds like an invitation, listen carefully. Is it a real invitation or is the person just being friendly?

Choose the right answer:

(　　) 1. Why do Canadians and Americans often invite friends for meals at home?

A. Because they can save time.

B. Because they can spend less money.

C. Because they enjoy entertaining at home.

D. Because they have modern and beautiful houses.

( ) 2. Which of the following is a real invitation?

A. "If you are free, let's go for a drink sometime. "

B. "Please go to the cinema with me some day. "

C. "Would you like to have a cup of tea with us sometime?"

D. "I have two tickets here. Can you go to the concert with me?"

( ) 3. If people say "Let's get together for lunch some day", you just say "_____"

A. That would be fine.   B. How about this weekend?

C. Oh, sorry. I'm very busy.   D. That's great. I'll be there on time.

( ) 4. People use "an unreal invitation" in order to show that _____.

A. they are trying to be friendly

B. they are trying to be helpful

C. they are trying to make friends with others

D. they haven't got ready for a party yet

( ) 5. The passage is mainly about _____.

A. entertainment at home

B. real invitations or not

C. expressions of starting a conversation

D. ways of ending a conversation

17

New rules and behavior standards for middle school students came out in March. Middle school is going to use a new way to decide who the top students are. The best students won't only have high marks, they will also be kids who don't dye their hair, smoke or drink. The followings are some of the new rules.

Tell the truth: Have you ever copied someone else's work in an exam? Don't do it again! That's not something an honest student should do. If you have played computer games for two hours in your room, don't tell your parents you have done homework.

Do more at school. Good students are kind to other people and love animals. April is bird-loving month in China. Is your school doing anything to celebrate? You should join! In that way, you can learn more about animals and how to protect them. When more people work together, it makes it more fun for everyone.

Have you ever quarreled with your teammates when your basketball team lost? Only working together can make your team stronger. Be friendly to the people you are with. Try to think of others, not only yourself.

Be open to new ideas. Have you ever thought that people could live on the moon? Maybe you'll discover Earth Ⅱ some day. Don't look down on new ideas. Everyone's ideas are important. You should welcome them, because new ideas make life better for everyone.

Protect yourself. Has someone ever taken money from one of your classmates? Don't let it happen to you. If you have to go home late, you should take care of yourself and let your parents know.

Use the Internet carefully. The Internet can be very useful for your studies. But some things on the Internet aren't for kids, so try to look at Web pages that are good for you. You can use the Web for fun or homework. Can't you find any good Websites for children? Here are some: http://kids. eastday. com; http://www. chinakids. net. com

Choose the right answer:

(　　) 1. An honest student should _____.

    A. tell the truth, even when you are young.

    B. copy someone else's work in an exam

    C. try to think of others, not only yourself

    D. quarrel with your teammates when your team lost

(　　) 2. The main idea of the fourth paragraph is about _____.

    A. making the team stronger　　　B. being strict with others

    C. learning from each other　　　D. working together with others

(　　) 3. The school new rules tell students to _____.

    A. live on the moon　　　B. discover Earth Ⅱ

    C. look down on new ideas　　　D. be open to new ideas

(　　) 4. Good Websites for children can _____.

    A. be a waste of time　　　B. make life much easier

    C. help them with their studies　　　D. do homework for them

(　　) 5. The school new rules will help kids by telling them _____.

    A. how they can study well

    B. what is right and what is wrong

    C. what they should do only at school

    D. how they can protect themselves

18

To master a language one must be able to speak and understand the spoken language as well as to read and write. Lenin and his wife translated a long English book into Russian, but when they went to England in 1902, English people couldn't understand a word Lenin and his wife said, and Lenin and his wife couldn't understand what was said to them. This shows the importance of spoken language.

Speaking, of course, can't go without listening. If you want to pronounce a word correctly, first you must hear it correctly. The sounds of Chinese and English languages are not exactly the same. If you don't listen carefully, you'll find it difficult or even impossible to understand the native speakers.

Well, what about writing? Like speaking, it's to exchange ideas. People usually use shorter words and shorter sentences in their writing.

The important thing is to make your idea clear in your mind and then to write it in a clear lively language.

Chinese students read too slowly. If you read fast, you will understand better. If you read too slowly, by the time you have reached to the end of a page you have forgotten what the beginning is about. When you meet with new words, don't look them up in the dictionary. Guess the meaning from the context(上下文). You may not guess quite correctly the first time, but as new words appear again and again in different context, their meaning will become clearer and clearer. If you look up every word, you'll never finish a book.

Students of a foreign language need a particular knowledge, the knowledge of life, history and geography of the people whose language they're studying. They should study those subjects in the foreign language, not only in translation. In this way one can kill two birds with one stone: learn a foreign language and get some knowledge of the foreign country at the same time.

Choose the right answer:

(   ) 1. In England, Lenin _____.

    A. could be understood by Englishmen

    B. could understand Englishmen

    C. and Englishmen couldn't understand each other

    D. and Englishmen could understand each other

(   ) 2. In the first paragraph the writer told us _____.

    A. how to speak English

    B. how to read and write

    C. why English people couldn't understand the Lenins

    D. why spoken English is important

(   ) 3. In the fifth paragraph the writer advised us on _____.

    A. how to guess the meaning of the words

    B. how to read fast

    C. how to look up new words in the dictionary

D. how to read carefully

( ) 4. The underlined "kill two birds with one stone" means _____.

A. to get more than what one pays

B. to get some particular knowledge

C. the stone is very useful

D. the birds are blind enough

( ) 5. In the last paragraph the writer advised us _____.

A. to kill two birds with one stone

B. to learn two languages at the same time

C. to study all the subjects in a foreign language

D. to get some knowledge of the foreign country whose language we are studying

19

Pat Brown went to her bank to ask for an ATM card. It looks like a credit card. A few weeks later, the bank posted her a card and a four number personal identification number(PIN). Her PIN is 1234.

As Pat was getting ready for bed one night, she remembered that she had only $2 in her bag. The next day she had to give $10 for a lunch for a co-worker. She didn't want to get up early to go to the bank. So she had to go to the bank that night. She used her ATM card to withdraw(take out) $50 from her checking account.

These are the steps she followed to withdraw money. First, she put her card in the lower slot(狭孔) on the right side of the machine. She made sure her card was facing the right way. Second, the computer screen(window) said, "Please enter(put in) your PIN." Pat pressed the numbers 1,2,3 and 4. Next, the screen said, "Please select type of transaction(交易) you want by pressing other keys." Pat pressed the bottom key for withdrawing money.

Then the screen said, "From which account?" The choices it gave were Checking, Saving, and Money market. Pat pressed the key for Checking. Next, the screen said, "Please select(choose) amount of transaction." Pat pushed the number 5 and then 0 three times, until the screen read, "50.00." The screen then read, "Please wait." In less than a minute it read, "Please lift(put up) the lid and take your money."

Pat lifted the lid marked Withdraw. She counted her $50 to make sure the ATM hadn't made a mistake. Then she waited for her withdrawal slip to come out of the slot at the upper right corner of the machine. Pat checked the slip to make sure it was correct. Then her ATM card was returned through the card slot. She put it in her bag and walked away. If Pat had made a mistake at any point by pressing the wrong button (number)，she could have pressed Cancel and started over again.

Choose the right answer：

(   ) 1. What was Pat's first step?

    A. Pressing the withdrawal button.

    B. Inserting(putting into) her ATM card.

    C. Counting her money.

    D. Getting her withdrawal slip.

(   ) 2. What did Pat do immediately after choosing the account?

    A. Selected whether to withdraw, deposit, or transfer money.

    B. Selected the amount of money she wanted to withdraw.

    C. Got away her ATM card.

    D. Lifted the lid and removed her money.

(   ) 3. When did Pat enter her PIN?

    A. Right after inserting her card.

    B. Right before selecting the account.

    C. Right before selecting the amount of money.

    D. Right after selecting withdrawal.

(   ) 4. When did Pat select the type of transaction?

    A. Right after selecting which account she wants.

    B. Right before receiving her withdrawal slip.

    C. Right before selecting the amount.

    D. Right after recording her PIN.

(   ) 5. What did Pat do when the screen said，"Please lift the lid..."?

    A. Got out her card.

    B. Selected the type of transaction she wanted.

    C. Took her $50.

    D. Picked up her withdrawal slip.

20

Problems on travelling are often found very difficult in the arithmetic(算术) competition for elementary pupils. However, complicated problems can sometimes be settled in a very simple way.

Example　Tom and Mary start at the same time walking towards each other from two separate places A and B. If they walk at a set normal(正常的) speed, they will meet in 4 hours. But if they each walk 1 000 metres an hour slower, they meet in 5 hours. What is the distance between A and B?

Analysis　Let's suppose Tom and Mary are walking at the lower speed, that is, one thousand meters an hour slower than normal, and keep walking 4 hours. Of course they cannot meet, and now the distance between them is CD. CD is exactly the distance they should have covered if they each had walked one kilometer an hour faster. So CD=1 000 (m/h)×4(h)×2 =8 000(m). They cover the distance in another hour, and think that they finish the whole journey in 5 hours. Sure you can easily get the distance AB. Don't you think?

Exercise　Jack and Jane live in two cities, E and F. Every Saturday morning they drive their cars towards each other from home at 7:00 am. They will meet exactly after a three-hour ride. But one day Jack's car breaks down and he has to drive a tractor instead, which runs 20 kilometres slower in an hour. This time, they meet at 10:30 am. The question is: how far apart are City E and City F?

Choose the right answer:

(　　) 1. The passage above may be taken from _____.

    A. a copy of *China Daily*

    B. a teachers' book for elementary English

    C. an arithmetic training course

    D. a travel book

(　　) 2. The underlined word "complicated" in the first paragraph means _____.

    A. very easy to deal with   B. impossible to work out

    C. interesting to settle   D. difficult to understand

(　　) 3. The distance between A and B is _____.

    A. 8 000 metres   B. 32 000 metres

    C. 40 000 metres   D. 48 000 metres

(　　) 4. The distance between City E and City F is _____ kilometres.

    A. 420   B. 360   C. 490   D. 280

(　　) 5. What can we learn from the passage?

    A. All the travelling problems can be worked out in the way above.

    B. Arithmetic problems are always more interesting than puzzling.

    C. Arithmetic problems can often be settled in different ways.

    D. Simple methods will surely work in dealing with every travelling problem.

第二部分 主观阅读理解

一、题型特点：

主观阅读是阅读理解的一种形式，它不仅考查学生对文章的理解，还考查了学生的语言表达能力，近几年根据新课标的要求出现的任务型阅读更是主观阅读的一个趋势。

二、题型分类：

主观阅读相对于客观阅读题型丰富，形式多样，可以从多种角度考察学生的语言知识和理解能力。常见的主要有以下几种形式：

 题型一:根据短文内容回答下面的问题。

解题指导：

对于回答问题这种类型的题目，除了做一般阅读理解要遵循的步骤外还要注意下面的解题技巧：

1. 细读题目，明确问题。

浏览全文后要将问题仔细分析，明确各题需要我们解决什么问题，千万不可"答非所问"。

2. 注意几种问题的类型。

虽然是根据文章回答问题，但也要注意问题的类型各不相同。

（1）细节理解题：往往用 what,who,how,where,why,when 等特殊疑问词来引导，对文章某一段落中某一细节进行提问。

（2）文章主旨的理解题:此类题目用来检查我们对文章主题和中心思想的理解是否正确。在具体考察中往往要求我们概括文章的标题或是主旨。

（3）单词或句子的翻译题:此类题目要将单词和句子带到文章中去，根据上下文来猜测词意，切不可"断章取义"。

3. 答案写下后要复读文章，检查答案。

解答完各题后应再复读文章，核对答案。对于写下的答案还要检查有没有单词或语法错误，真正做到"万无一失"。同时还要做到书写整洁。

典型例题

Jim, a successful businessman, told the experience of his childhood.

When he was 12, his parents died. He was alone and didn't get on well with others. People always laughed at him. No one showed kindness to him.

His only friend was a dog named Tige. He gave his dog enough to eat and drink, but sometimes he was not friendly to it. He didn't know that an unkind word sometimes could cut one's heart like a knife.

One day as he walked down the street, a young lady was walking in front of him. Suddenly one of her bags dropped from her arms. As she stopped to pick it up, she dropped other bags. He came to help her. "Thank you, dear! You are a nice little boy!" She said kindly, smiling.

A special feeling came to him. It was the first time that he had heard such kind words. He watched her until she went far away, and then he whistled(吹口哨)to his dog and went directly to the river nearby.

"Thank you, dear! You are a nice little boy!" He repeated what the woman said. Then in a low voice he said to his dog, "You are a nice little dog." Tige raised its ears as if it understood.

"Hmm! Even a dog likes it!" he said. "Well, Tige, I won't say anything unkind to you any more." Tige waved its tail happily.

The boy thought and thought. Finally he looked at himself in the river. He saw nothing but a dirty boy. He washed his face carefully. Again he looked. He saw a clean nice boy. He was amazed. From then on, he started a new life.

After telling this, the businessman stopped for a while, and then he said, "Ladies and gentlemen, **this is the very place in which that kind woman planted the first seed(种子) of kindness in my heart.** All of us should learn about kindness. What a great power it has!"

1. Why did nobody show kindness to Jim?

   _____

2. Who was Jim's friend?

   _____

3. Jim didn't start his new life after meeting the young lady, did he?

   _____

4. Put the sentence "This is the very place in which that kind woman planted the first seed(种子) of kindness in my heart." into Chinese.

   _____

5. What's the best title of this passage?

【答案与解析】

1. **Because he didn't get on well with others.** 由文章第二小节的"He was alone and didn't get on well with others. No one showed kindness to him."可知。

2. **His dog. / A dog named Tige. / Tige.** 根据文章第三小节的"His only friend was a dog named Tige."可知。

3. **Yes, he did. / Yes.** 理解为"不,他开始了新的生活。"文章的主体部分主要是讲这个男孩因为这位年轻女士的一句表扬在生活态度上有了很大的转变,文章倒数第二小节提到"From then on, he started a new life."这里的 then 就是指 after meeting the young lady。

4. 就是在这个地方,那位善良的妇女在我心里播下了第一颗善良的种子。 要准确翻译这句话要特别注意这里有一个定语从句,in which 这里就是指 in the very place。还要注意这里的 very place 要翻译为"就是这个地方"。

5. **The Power of Kindness.** 要设好一个标题关键要抓住文章的主旨,这篇文章的关键点就是 kindness 给小男孩带来的巨大的精神力量,而且文章的最后一段也揭示了文章的主旨。

实战演练

1

Jeff Keith has only one leg. When he was 12 years old, Jeff had a cancer. The doctors had to cut off most of his right leg to save his life. Every day Jeff puts on an artificial man-made leg. The leg is plastic(塑料的). With the plastic leg, Jeff can ski, ride a bicycle, swim and play soccer. He also can run.

When he was 22 years old, Jeff ran across the United States, from the East to the West. He ran 5 150 kilometers, that's about 26 kilometers each day. Jeff wore out 36 pairs of running shoes and five plastic legs.

On his way, in every city people gave Jeff money. The money which Jeff received was not for Jeff himself. It was for the American Cancer Society(协会). The Society used the money to learn more about cancer. At the same time, Jeff talked to people about cancer. He also talked about being disabled.

Jeff is disabled, but he can do many things: skiing, swimming, playing soccer and running. He finished college and now he is studying to be a lawyer(律师). Jeff says, "People can do anything they want to do. I want people to know that. **I ran not only for disabled people but also for everybody.**"

1. Why did the doctors cut off most of Jeff's right leg?

2. Translate the sentence "I ran not only for disabled people but also for everybody." into Chinese.

_____

3. What did Jeff talk to the people on his way from the East to the West?

_____

4. How many plastic legs did Jeff wear out when he ran across the United States?

_____

5. What can we learn from the story?

_____

2

Television has now come to nearly every family. It has become a very important part in people's life. School children in some cities watch TV about twenty hours a week.

Some people believe that television is good for children because it helps them learn about their country and the world. With the help of programmes of education, children do better in school.

Other people feel that there are too many programmes about love and crime on TV, and that even programmes of education don't help children a lot. Children simply watch too much television, so they don't do a lot of other important things for their education.

Children of three to six learn to speak their own language and talk with people. When they are watching TV, they are only listening to the language, and they aren't talking with anyone. When school children watch TV, they read less. Because of this they don't learn to read or write quickly at school. All children learn by doing, and they need time to play in order to learn about the world. When they watch TV, they play less. They also have less time to do with their parents and friends, and they have less time to have sports.

Recently, a hundred and fifteen families in a middle school decided to stop watching TV for a month or more. At first it was difficult, but there were soon a lot of good changes. The children read, played, and exercised more and the family became full of joy. But at the end of the month all the families began to watch TV as much as before. No family was able to give up television completely.

1. Why does television become a very important part for school children in some cities?

_____

2. According to this article, what good things do television programmes help

children to learn about?

_____

3. Give the two reasons against children's watching TV in Paragraph 3.

_____

4. It is true that all children learn by doing. What do children need to do for their healthy personal growth?

_____

5. What is the best title for this passage(短文)?

_____

（2008 白下区一模卷）

3

Last week, 169 Junior One students at No. 35 Middle School of Shenyang took their first no-teacher exam. After the teacher handed out the exam papers, he left the room and never came back. A student collected the papers when the exam was over.

"That test was not only a test of knowledge, but also a test of morality(道德). We wanted to show the students how important honesty(诚实) is, " said Cai Wenguo, the school's headmaster. The school says no cheating(作弊) happened in the test. Next year, it wants 80% of its exams to be without teachers. But students have different ideas.

"I was happy and excited during the exam because my teachers trusted(信任) me, " said Lang Yudan, a 15-year-old girl in Class 11.

"Schools must trust students a lot and do not use invigilators(监考人) **in exams.** But I think it is too early. Some students will cheat if there are no invigilators. And the students will not be able to ask for help when they need, " said Hua Nan.

"I don't like having invigilators in exams. When they walk around the classroom, they make me nervous. I would get higher marks without them in the room because I would feel more relaxed. " Liu Qingxi said.

"I think it's very important to have invigilators in exams. Many students want to check their answers with each other after they have finished papers. And they can also keep the classroom in order when something unusual happens. They may make me nervous, but I still think we need them. " Shang Yuan said.

No-teacher exams may be a good idea. But before using them, schools must tell students the importance of honesty and try to find ways to solve something unusual in exams.

1. Why did No. 35 Middle School of Shenyang hold a no-teacher exam?

_____

2. How many students with disagreement are mentioned in this passage?

_____

3. What does Hua Nan think about no-teacher exams?

_____

4. What does the underlined word "them" in the sentence refer to(指代)?

_____

5. Translate the sentence "Schools must trust students a lot and do not use invigilators in exams." into Chinese.

_____

(2008 鼓楼区二模卷)

4

Don and his 11-year-old son, Aaron, love basketball. For Aaron's birthday last October, Don decided to take him to Cincinnati, more than two hours' drive, for the first game of the World Series(世界联赛). They had no tickets but hoped to buy a pair from scalpers(票贩子).

After arriving, they walked in the streets for two hours, carrying a sign that said, "We need two tickets." There were a lot of scalpers, but the cheapest ticket was $175. They were about to leave when a man stopped them. He took out two tickets and gave them to the father. "How much do you want?" Don asked, "No charge(收费)," said the man. "Enjoy the game."

When asked later, the man explained, "I am working for Joe, who hasn't missed a World Series in the past 16 years. But he is ill and can't watch the game this time. So he told me to give the two tickets away. He asked me to give the tickets to the right people. A lot of people looked as if they might just take the tickets and sell them. Then I saw you. You seemed very <u>disappointed</u> and you made me think of my dad and me when I was a child. I wanted very much to go to a World Series game with my father. But I never did."

How important was it to Don and his son? Here is what Don said, "It's the most memorable(值得纪念的) thing that has ever happened to us. My boy and I turned to each other 30 times during the game and said, 'I can't believe this.' We'll never forget that day."

1. Why did Don decide to take his son, Aaron, to Cincinnati?

_____

2. Did Don and Aaron buy tickets from scalpers?

_____

3. Why did Joe ask the man to give the two tickets away?

4. Did Joe love to watch the World Series?

_____

5. What does the underlined word "disappointed" mean in Chinese?   (   )
   A. 兴奋的   B. 疯狂的   C. 失望的   D. 顽皮的

（2008 高淳县二模卷）

5

A superstar is someone who is unusually famous in sports, films, or popular music, someone like the singer Zhou Jielun.

The word "super" means more than usual or very wonderful. And of course, a "star" is a person who is very famous and skillful. So the top people who are very wonderful and skillful in sports, films or music are called superstars, such as Li Ning.

One of the most famous sports superstars in the United States is the boxer named Ali. After he won a gold medal in the Olympics and became the heavy-weight boxing champion, **he was known as one of the greatest and most famous boxers in the sports history.**

At that time Ali was even better known than the president of the United States. He was a true superstar. Nearly everyone knew his name.

But like the stars in the sky, a superstar, may disappear as the years go by. These days people know little about Ali.

Superstars, loved by millions of people today, maybe will be forgotten tomorrow.

1. What is a superstar?

_____

2. What's the Chinese for "boxing champion"?

_____

3. Can superstars be remembered forever?

_____

4. 请写出"These days people know little about Ali."的同义句。

_____

5. Translate the sentence "he was known as one of the greatest and most famous boxers in the sports history" into Chinese.

_____

6

Thanksgiving Day is a very special day for people in the United States. They celebrate it on the last Thursday in November. Canadians also celebrate Thanksgiving

Day, but they do it on the second Monday of October. In Britain, where this festival is called "Harvest Festival", people celebrate it earlier in the year, in September.

A harvest is the fruit you take from the trees and the crops you take from the ground. In North America and Britain, harvest time for most fruit and crops is in the autumn. In these countries and other Christian places, people give thanks to God on a special day of the year. **They thank God for the good things that have happened during the year and for the good harvest they have had.** People usually take small boxes of fruit, flowers and vegetables to their churches to show their thanks.

The first thanksgiving service(仪式)in North America took place on December 4th, 1619 when 38 English people arrived in America to make their home in the new country. They held this service not to thank God for the harvest, but to thank God for their safe journey. The next year, many more English people arrived. They had a bad winter, but fortunately the harvest was good. They decided to celebrate it with a big meal. They shot and killed small animals to eat and cooked everything outside on large fires. About 90 Indians also came to the meal. Everyone ate at tables outside their houses and played games together. The festival lasted three days.

A Thanksgiving Day celebration was held every year for a long time, but not always on the same day of the year. Then, in 1789, President George Washington named November 26th as the Day of Thanksgiving. In 1863, President Abraham Lincoln changed the date, and said that the last Thursday in November should be Thanksgiving Day.

1. Is Thanksgiving Day celebrated on the same day in North American countries?

_____

2. When did the first thanksgiving service take place in North America?

_____

3. Who made the last Thursday in November Thanksgiving Day in the USA?

_____

4. What does the underlined word "fortunately" mean in Chinese?

_____

5. Translate the sentence "They thank God for the good things that have happened during the year and for the good harvest they have had." into Chinese.

_____

7

For several years, Americans have enjoyed teleshopping—watching TV and buying things by phone. Now, teleshopping is starting in Europe. In a number of European countries, people can turn on their TVs and shop for clothes, jewelry, food, toys and many other things.

Teleshopping is becoming popular in Sweden. For example, the biggest Swedish company sells different kinds of things on TV in 15 European countries, and in one year it made $100 million. In France, there are two teleshopping channels, and the French spend $20 million a year to buy things through those channels.

In Germany, until last year teleshopping was only possible on one channel for one hour every day. Then the government allowed more teleshopping. Other channels can open for telebusiness, including teleshopping companies. German businesses are hoping this new teleshopping will help them sell more things.

Some people like teleshopping because it allows them to do their shopping without leaving their homes. With all the problems of traffic in the cities, this is an important reason. But at the same time, other Europeans do not like this new way of shopping. The call teleshopping "junk(垃圾)on the air". Many Europeans usually worry about the quality of the things for sale on TV. Good quality is important to them, and they believe they can't be sure of the quality of the things on TV.

The need for high quality means that European teleshopping companies will have to be different from the American companies. They will have to be more careful about the quality of the things they sell. They will also have to work harder to sell things that the buyers can't touch or see in person.

1. What is teleshopping?

_____

2. In Europe, how many countries have already started teleshopping?

_____

3. Is teleshopping more popular in Germany or in France?

_____

4. Why do some Europeans prefer teleshopping?

_____

5. What is the most important to the European buyers?

_____

8

A farm is always a busy place. One of the busiest things is when the farmer is getting land ready to grow plants.

If the farmer is going to grow wheat, he has to turn the ground over first. The farmer drives up and down the paddock on tractor. When the ground is ready, the farmer sows the seeds. He does this with a machine that the tractor pulls along. Now, one farmer and one machine can do as much a day as twenty men used to do without a machine. After the wheat has been sown, the farmer keeps a lookout for rain. Wheat needs rain and warm sunny days to make it grow. When the wheat has grown, it turns to a lovely golden colour.

When the wheat is fully grown, you can see the seeds on the wheat plants. These have to be cut off and put in bags or big trucks to be taken to a factory where they are made into flour.

It's a very busy time on farm when the wheat is being cut. Everyone helps so that all the wheat can be taken from the paddocks before the rain comes. If heavy rain falls, the farmer must wait for the ground dry out before the machine can cut the wheat. Farmers always have a lot to do through the year.

1. What is the busiest thing?

_____

2. What does the farmer have to do if he is going to grow wheat?

_____

3. Why was much more time spent on sowing in the past?

_____

4. What don't farmers need when they cut wheat?

_____

5. Does everyone help to cut the wheat?

_____

9

John Brown, an office worker, lives in Washington. He inherited(继承) $1 000 000 when he was 23. He didn't feel happy at all. His college friends were looking for their first jobs, but he didn't have to. John decided to keep living a simple life like everyone else. He didn't tell any of his friends and gave $100 000 of his money to a charity that helped poor children to live better lives. Today he is 36, he still wears cheap shoes and clothes and owns a small car only, but he is much happier.

Up to now John had helped 15 children from poor countries all over the world, $200 a month for each. The child does not receive the money in cash(现金). The money pays for the child's school expenses, food, medical care and clothing. John receives a report each year on the child's progress. They can write to each other, but usually the children do not speak English.

When John first heard about these children, he wanted to help them. "It was not anything special," he said. "Until I had the chance to go to these countries and meet the children I was helping, I did not know anything about the type of life they had."

Once John went to meet a little girl in Africa. He said that the meeting was very exciting. "When I met her, I felt very, very happy," he said. "I saw that the money was used for a very good plan. It brought me closer to the child in a way that giving money alone cannot. " "I want to do everything I can. I will go on helping these children in need," he added.

根据短文内容回答下列问题

1. What kind of life is John living?

2. Did he want to look for a job or stay at home after he got the money?

3. Does John only help the poor children in Africa?

4. The child receives the money in cash, doesn't he?

5. Why did John say that the meeting with the little girl was exciting?

10

Specialists in marketing have studied how to make people buy more food in a supermarket. They do all kinds of things that you do not even notice. For example, the simple, ordinary food that everybody must buy, like bread, milk, flour and vegetable oil, is spread all over the store. You have to walk by all the more interesting and more expensive things in order to find what you need. The more expensive food is in packages with brightly colored pictures. This food is placed at eye level so you see it and want to buy it. The things that you have to buy anyway are usually located on a higher or lower shelf. However, chocolate and other things that children like are on lower shelves. One study showed that when a supermarket moved four products from the floor to eye level, it sold 78 percent more.

Another study showed that for every minute a person is in a supermarket after the first half hour, she or he spends $50. If someone stays forty minutes, the supermarket has additional $5.00. So the store has a comfortable temperature in summer and winter, and it plays soft music. It is a pleasant place for people to stay and spend more money.

1. Where is the simple and ordinary food in a supermarket?

2. What do specialists in marketing do with the more expensive food?

3. Where can children find chocolate and other things they like?

4. How can a supermarket increase sales?

5. People don't spend more money in a pleasant supermarket, don't they?

_____

 题型二:根据短文内容用恰当的单词或短语完成下面的表格。

解题指导:

1. 此题型往往设计成各式各样的表格形式,要求学生根据文章的内容用适当的单词或短语来完成这些表格。其实这些表格正体现了整篇文章的基本结构,所以只要对文章的基本结构理解了完成起来并不难。

2. 基本都是细节题,绝大多数答案都能在文中直接找到。只要能认真阅读文章,找到关键句就很容易找到答案了。

3. 要特别注意题目中一些句式的变化。同样意思的句子,在题目中换一种说法,考验学生还能不能准确找出关键词。所以要真正理解句子的意思。

4. 有些答案并不能在文章中直接找到,需要学生根据句意用自己的语言来组织。这是比较难的。这时要仔细推敲,结合上下文去进行概括和总结,从而做出准确的判断。

典型例题

根据短文内容,完成下面的表格:

A map is a picture of a place. There can be many different maps of the same place. A map can't show everything about a place. For a clear map, it must show a number of things. Here, you will get to make a map which shows the things that make your community(社区) a special place to live in.

Before you start drawing, make a list of the places and things in your community that you want to include on your map. Think about places you often have to go to, places where your relatives and friends live and your favourite places. How do you get there? What roads or paths do you take? What kind of things do you see along the way? As you know, some maps are made to show locations and other maps show us how to get there. They can also show the distances.

Now, let's create a map of your community. On a large piece of paper, draw pictures of the places or the things you decide to include on your map. Next, fill in the shapes of the places and roads in light colours. Using darker colours, fill in the areas between the features and roads on your map to make your map more interesting to look at. Every area of your map should be filled in with colours. When your map is finished, show it to your friends or family members to see what they think of it.

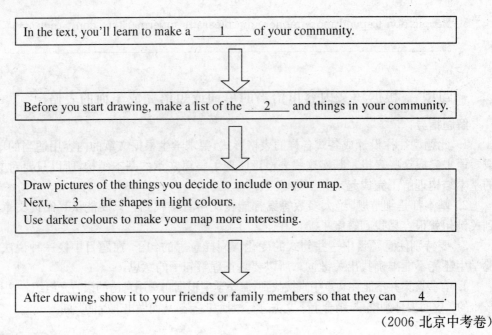

In the text, you'll learn to make a ____1____ of your community.

Before you start drawing, make a list of the ____2____ and things in your community.

Draw pictures of the things you decide to include on your map.
Next, ____3____ the shapes in light colours.
Use darker colours to make your map more interesting.

After drawing, show it to your friends or family members so that they can ____4____.

(2006 北京中考卷)

【答案与解析】

1. **map**　　根据文章第一小节这句话"Here，you will get to make a map which shows the things that make your community(社区) a special place to live in."可知。

2. **places**　　根据文章第二小节这句话"Before you start drawing，make a list of the places and things in your community that you want to include on your map."可知。

3. **fill in**　　根据文章最后一小节这句话"Next，fill in the shapes of the places and roads in light colours."可知。

4. **give their advice/suggestions/opinions**　　根据文章最后一句话"When your map is finished，show it to your friends or family members to see what they think of it."可知此题没有直接答案，需要自己根据句意重新组织语言，有一定难度。

实战演练

1

When the idea of going to Beirut(贝鲁特) first came to my mind in 2001，I thought something was going wrong with me. I had always thought Beirut was a war-torn(战争创伤的) place with rude and hungry people running all over. But I was wrong.

The airport in Beirut was just like any airport you could find in Canada and the United States. Everything was clean and new. The people there were very helpful and very kind.

The streets of Beirut were not what I had expected. I thought it would be a terrible place with broken buildings and things of that kind. Instead I saw a beautiful city with tall buildings and busy streets filled with laughing people who were very friendly and understanding of my foreign ways.

I thought that their way of life, their clothes and their food would be different. I was right about one thing—their food was different but it was amazing. However, they have different kinds of western foods and western restaurants. Their clothing is exactly the same. Their language is beautiful and they live a happy life. English and French are widely spoken. I have visited Beirut four times after that and I plan to go there again.

Fill in the table below:

	Streets	People	Food	Clothing
Beirut in the writer's mind	1. _____	2. _____	Different	Different
Beirut in the writer's eyes	Busy	3. _____	4. _____	5. _____

2

Good evening, ladies and gentlemen. Welcome to the Richmond Film Society. Tonight, we begin a season of Marilyn Monroe films. Before we start the film I'd like to say just a few words about Marilyn Monroe's life.

Marilyn was born in Los Angeles in 1926, but had quite a sad life as a child. Her father didn't want to see her from the time she was born and her mother became ill when she was very young and stayed in hospital for a long period of time. Between 1926 and 1935, Marilyn lived with lots of different families.

In 1935, she went to a school for girls with no parents, but didn't like it and left in 1942 when she married Jim Dougherty. In 1949 she met the famous film director Johnny Hyde, and in 1950 she made her first film, *The Asphalt Jungle*.

Between 1950 and 1961 she made thirty-one films. She was, however, never very happy. She died in Hollywood in 1962.

Personal Information

Name: Marilyn Monroe   Birthplace: 1

Nationality: American   Age of the first marriage: 2

Name of her first film: 3

Achievements 1950~1961: 4

Age of death: 5

---

1. _____   2. _____   3. _____   4. _____   5. _____

3

Welcome to England! The weather of England is very changeable. It can be rainy, sunny, cloudy, windy, warm, foggy or cold at any time of year. If it's raining when you get up in the morning, it can be hot and dry by the afternoon. The west of England is wetter than the east, and the north is cooler than the south. Just be ready for any kind of weather.

In England, shops are usually open from 9:00 in the morning to 5:30 in the afternoon. On Sundays some shops are open from 10:00 to 4:00. But a lot of shops are closed. Banks, museums or other places are open from 10:00 am to 5:00 pm. You can go to the parks at any time.

All the cities have buses, trains and taxis. People wait in line for buses and they are unhappy if you push in at the front. Don't forget this, traffic goes on the left. Be careful!

Notice to the Tourists

* Just be ready for any kind of ___1___. It's changeable.
* Shops are usually open from ___2___. On Sundays most of them are closed.
* At any time you can go to the ___3___.
* Please ___4___ when you are at the bus stop.
* Make sure not walk on the ___5___ of the road, or it will be very dangerous.

---

1. _____   2. _____   3. _____   4. _____   5. _____

4

How good projects grow

Are you interested in projects(项目，课题) and do you want to have a good one? Well, that doesn't come easily. You need to do the following tasks:

TALK: You and your classmates discuss in detail all that you would like to do to realize your project.

WRITE: One of your classmates acts as(担任)a secretary. He or she keeps full notes as your group discusses. Later he or she will sort(整理) your ideas to make them better.

PLAN: With the secretary's notes, your group makes a list of everything you'll need and who will get, do or research what.

DO: Each group member gets, does and researches something on the list. Your group puts together all you have found and tries to make the project more well-organized. You prepare to present it in class.

SHOW: You and your classmates show the world the result of your hard work.

Knowing all the above, you may want to try a project. Why not start with this:

Can you find out more about the history of your city? What did it look like? Which famous people lived there?

根据短文内容,用单词或不超过5个单词的短语完成下面的表格。

To grow good projects	Talk	Discuss everything ___1___ .
	Write	The secretary should ___2___ while you are discussing.
	Plan	___3___ of your needs and make everyone's task clear.
	Do	Do the research work and make the project ___4___ .
	Show	Show ___5___ to the world.

1. _____   2. _____   3. _____   4. _____   5. _____

5

Charles Dickens was born in 1812 in one of the small towns of England.

When Dickens was nine years old, his father found a job in London and the family moved there. Later on, his father was put into prison for owing(负债). His mother could not supply enough food to him and his younger brothers and sisters. He had to do something for his family. He did some housework and looked after his brothers and sisters. Their life was so hard that he could not go to school.

Only until his father was out of prison could Charles go to school. At that time he was already twelve. But he did not finish school. Two years later he began to work in a factory.

And he was a journalist and wrote for newspapers. The future writer often went to the library to read books. He read a lot. Then, at the age of twenty-two, Dickens began to write and he wrote a lot of novels and stories all his life. Dickens died over a hundred years ago, but people are still reading his books with great interest.

根据文章完成下面的表格。

Time	Things happened to Charles Dickens
___1___ years old	moved to London
Later on	could not go to school
When he was 12	his father was ___2___ ___3___ prison
In ___4___	he began to work in a factory
At the age of 22	he began to ___5___

1. _____   2. _____   3. _____   4. _____   5. _____

题型三:根据短文内容用恰当的单词将下面的文章补充完整。

解题指导:

要解好这类题,注意遵循以下步骤:

1. 浏览全文,了解大意。

2. 根据题目,细读相关段落和句子。

3. 理解关键句子的含义,找出关键词作答。

4. 对于在关键句中不能直接找到答案的问题,要根据原文和问题所在的句子进行仔细推敲,有时可以借助一些句型,推断出答案,这一点在下面的"典型例题"中有所体现。

5. 全部填完后要将改写的文章整体再读一遍,检查答案,看看文章是否连贯。

典型例题

Olympic torch relay around the world

The Beijing 2008 Olympic Torch Relay(火炬接力) will travel the longest distance, cover the greatest area and include the largest number of people. On March 25, Olympic Flame(火种) will be lit(点燃) in Greece.

Route Distance: 137 000 km

Time: 130 days

Route: Torch Relay starts in Beijing ⟶ London ⟶ Paris ⟶ San Francisco ⟶ Hong Kong ⟶ Beijing

Torch Length: 72 cm

Torch Weight: 985 grams

Design: It is based on the shape of a paper scroll(卷) with lucky clouds on it. It can stay lighted(燃烧的) in bad weather conditions.

根据以上信息,每空填一词。

The Beijing 2008 Olympic Torch Relay will travel a _____ distance than before. It will take more than _____ months to travel around the world. The Torch Relay will start in the city of _____. The torch is _____ cm long and 985 grams heavy. It looks like a paper scroll. Bad weather can't _____ the torch from burning.

(2007 镇江市中考卷)

【答案与解析】

1. **longer** 根据文章的第一句话 The Beijing 2008 Olympic Torch Relay will travel the longest distance,要注意改写过的文章中提到"than before",所以这里要注意用比较级。

2. **four** 从 Time 可知"130 days",算一下是 4 个多月的时间。

3. **Beijing** 从 Route 可知从北京开始传递。这里要注意希腊是点燃火种的地方。

4. **72** 从 Torch Length 可知。

5. **stop/prevent/keep** 根据最后一句话"It can stay lighted in bad weather

conditions." 可知火炬可以在恶劣天气下保持燃烧,不会熄灭,所以可以用 stop/ prevent/ keep... from... 的句型来完成这个句子。

实战演练

1

Once there is an old farmer who has three sons. "To which one shall I leave my fortune(财富)?" he thinks. "It must be to the cleverest son. But which one is the cleverest?"

He calls his three sons to him. "Here is some money," he tells them. "You each must take one coin to buy something that will fill this room. The one who can buy something to fill this room shall have my fortune."

"It's a big room," says the oldest son.

"One coin will not buy very much," says the second son.

But the youngest son says nothing. He stands and thinks, and then he smiles, "Come on, brothers," he says. "Let us go to the market."

The oldest son buys straw(稻草) with his coin. But one coin buys only a bit of straw.

The second son buys sand with his coin. But one coin buys a bit of sand, too.

"What did you buy?" the oldest son asks the youngest son angrily. "You don't have any straw."

"Yes, what did you buy?" the second son asks angrily. "You don't have any sand."

"I bought this," says the youngest son.

"A candle!" cry his brothers, "What good is a candle?"

"Watch," says the youngest son. He lights the candle, and all at once the room is filled from wall to wall, from ceiling to floor. It is filled with light!

"Though you are the youngest, you are indeed the cleverest of my sons," their father says. "I'll give you all my fortune."

根据短文内容和首字母填空。

An old farmer has three sons and some f __1__. He decides to leave it to the c __2__ son. So he tells them to buy something with one coin to f __3__ the room. The oldest son and the second son both fail. However, the youngest son succeeds in doing it by lightening a c __4__. He fills the room with l __5__.

1. _____ 2. _____ 3. _____ 4. _____ 5. _____

2

From Bad Boy to Hero

Allen Iverson was once the troublemaker that the NBA did not want. He went to prison for fighting. He didn't like practising and he laughed at his coach(教练). But in the end, he hasn't wasted his talent.

At 1.83 metres tall, Iverson has become the most exciting player in the NBA. He's as quick as lightning and no one can stop him.

Over the years, he has also changed and become a leader. "If you're getting older and not getting smarter, something is wrong," said Iverson.

On November 6, he was named *the Eastern Conference Players of the Week*(本周东部最佳球员). He got the award for his play in the first week of the NBA. For his team, the Philadelphia 76ers(费城76人队), he scored an average(平均) of 34 points per game.

It was a proud moment for the 31-year-old player, especially since he has several injuries. Iverson has a fighting spirit and the heart of a giant.

Born to a single mum, Iverson grew up on dangerous streets in the US. Sometimes his house had no electricity, hot water or lights. There were only bills. He became tough like his friends.

But he knew he wouldn't win a championship or be on top with his bad behaviour. He looked at himself in the mirror and asked, "Who is Allen Iverson?" In this way he changed himself.

"I have matured," he said. "I'm proud that I recognize that. I'm trying to be a better person first, and then a better player."

根据短文内容和首字母提示填空。

Allen Iverson is a very famous basketball player in the NBA. But he was once a t __1__ and went to prison for fighting. But then he realized that he can't be successful with his bad b __2__ . Now, he has m __3__ and became a l __4__ of his team. Also, he realized he must try to be a better p __5__ first.

1. _____ 2. _____ 3. _____ 4. _____ 5. _____

3

There are 5 channels on British television and each channel has several news programmes throughout the day. Some programmes are only for 3 minutes but some are one hour long.

The people who read the news are called news presenters and because they appear on television every day, they are very famous.

There is a popular news presenter in England called Trevor McDonald, in the news studio. He presents a television programme called "News At Ten" every Monday to Friday evenings.

Another popular news presenter is Kirsty Young. She has a more modern style of reading the news and she likes sitting on a desk not on a chair! Television news presenters need to have worked as journalists(记者) because they have to write most of the news that they read. So they spend several hours in the news studio before their programme starts.

They decide, with the producer of the programme, what news events should be included. The presenters need to learn how to say any difficult words, like foreign names, and they look at news films that other journalists have sent to the studio.

Sometimes an important news event occurs after the programme has started so the presenter has to be able to read something without looking at it first. They must always keep calm when there are many changes during the programme. It's not easy, right?

根据短文内容填空。

In Britain, there are several news programmes on TV. The person called ___1___ appears on TV every day and becomes famous. Sometimes, the famous presenters don't like sitting on the chair, they have a more ___2___ style of reading the news—sitting on the ___3___! It's difficult to be a good a television news presenter in Britain. They need to ___4___ most of the news themselves, learn to say many difficult words and sometimes read the news ___5___ looking at it first.

1. _____   2. _____   3. _____   4. _____   5. _____

4

Good afternoon. Welcome to England. I hope that your visit will be a pleasant one. Today, I'd like to draw your attention to a few of our laws.

Firstly, I want to say something about drinking. Now you may not buy alcohol in this country if you are under 18 years old, nor may your friends buy it for you.

Secondly, noise. Enjoy yourselves by all means, but please don't make unnecessary noise, particularly at night. We ask you to respect other people who may wish to be quiet.

Thirdly, traffic. Be careful when you cross the road. The traffic moves on the left side of the road in our country. Use the crossing for walking and don't take any chances when you cross the road.

Fourthly, rubbish. It is against the law to throw away waste material in public places. When you have something to throw away, please put it in your pocket or in your bag and take it home, or put it in a rubbish bin.

If you need any kind of help, you can get in touch with the local police station. The police will be pleased to help you. Thank you.

根据短文内容用恰当的单词填空。

If you travel to England, there are a lot of rules for you to obey. In England, people ___1___ 18 can't buy alcohol. It is impolite to make a lot of ___2___, so enjoy yourselves in a proper way. Don't be surprised when you see the traffic moves on the ___3___ side of the road and take care while ___4___ the road. The last one, don't put rubbish anywhere. All the rubbish must be put in ___5___ or bags and take it home. If you have some trouble, please call the police.

1. _____   2. _____   3. _____   4. _____   5. _____

5

Mrs Bailey and her little daughter, Julie, were coming back home from shopping when they saw their neighbour, Mrs Perkins, standing outside her front door looking very upset(焦急不安的).

"Hello, what's the matter? You do look worried," said Mrs Bailey.

"I've done a silly thing. I've locked myself outside," said Mrs Perkins. "I don't know what to do. If I weren't so fat, I'd be able to get in through the window and open the door from the inside. That small window at the side of my house isn't fastened(闩住)."

Mrs Bailey thought for a moment and then asked Julie to climb through the window. Mrs Perkins wondered if Julie would be thin enough to unlock the door when she got in. Julie said she would try. So the two ladies helped the girl to climb in. They waited anxiously by the door, looking through the key hole.

They were very pleased when they heard Julie behind the door. She reached up and unlocked the door. Mrs Perkins pushed the door wide open and walked into her own home.

"Thanks a lot, Julie," said Mrs Perkins.

Mrs Bailey said that Mrs Perkins had been lucky this time but it was really not safe to leave the window open as thieves might get in.

"Only if they are thinner than I am!" replied Mrs Perkins.

根据文章内容用适当的单词填空：

Mrs Perkins was ___1___ when she found her keys were left in the house. She found a small window of the house was ___2___ fastened, but she was too ___3___ to get in through the window. Julie was thin enough to climb in through the window and ___4___ the door. Although Mrs Perkins was lucky this time, she must be careful because it is

_____5_____ to leave the windows open as thieves might get in the house.

1. _____　　2. _____　　3. _____　　4. _____　　5. _____

其他题型

除了上述三种常见题型外，主观阅读还有一些其他形式，下面的题目不妨试试看吧！

1

阅读文章，根据文章内容，完成句子。

The air around the earth is called atmosphere. It's up to more than 600 miles high. Airplanes fly only a few miles high in the air. The atmosphere makes the temperature on the earth so good that a great number of living things can stay alive.

Air is all around us. Air is a mixture of gases(气体) that we can not see. About one fifth of the air is oxygen, which is needed by all living things. About four fifths of the air is nitrogen(氮). Plants need it to live. There are other gases in the air. The most important among them is carbon dioxide. Green plants use carbon dioxide to make food. People give off carbon dioxide when they breathe.

Air has weight and takes up space. Air pressure(压力) inside our body is almost the same as air pressure outside. Because of this balance, we don't feel the pressure of the air on us.

Since the sun's heat affects the earth's air, the weather conditions on the earth change greatly: warm or hot; cool or cold; sunny or cloudy; windy, rainy, or snowy.

When temperature changes, what happens to the air? When air is being heated, it expands(膨胀). That means it takes up more space. When air is being cooled, it takes up less space, or contracts(收缩).

1. We call the air around the earth _____.

2. About twenty percent of the air is _____.

3. When people breathe, they give off _____, which is used to make food by green plants.

4. Although air has _____, we don't feel its pressure on us.

5. The weather on the earth is changeable because of _____.

6. When the air temperature gets higher, the air _____.

(2007 常州市中考卷)

2

Last Friday, after doing all the family shopping in town, I wanted to have a rest before catching the train. I bought a newspaper and some chocolate and went into the station coffee shop. It was a cheap self-service place with long tables to sit at. I put my heavy bag down on the floor, put the newspaper and chocolate on the table and then (A)去要一杯咖啡.

When I came back with the coffee, there was someone sitting in the next seat. It was a boy, with dark glasses and old clothes, and his hair was coloured bright red at the front. He had started to eat my chocolate!

Naturally, I was rather uneasy about him, but I didn't want to have any trouble. I just looked down at the front page of the newspaper, tasted my coffee and took a bit of chocolate. The boy looked at me closely. Then he took a second piece of my chocolate. I could hardly believe it. (B)Still I didn't say anything to him. When he took a third piece, I felt more angry than uneasy. I thought, "Well, I shall have the last piece." And I got (C)it.

The boy gave me a strange look, then stood up. As he left he shouted out, "There's something wrong with that woman!" Everyone looked at me, but I did not want to quarrel with the boy, so I kept quiet. I did not realize that I had made a mistake until I finished my coffee and was ready to leave. My face turned red when I saw my unopened chocolate (D) _____ the newspaper. The chocolate that I had been eating was the boy's!

1. 将(A)译成英语:_____.
2. 改写(B):Still I _____ _____ to him. (每空一词)
3. 文中能替代(C)的短语是_____。
4. 在(D)的空白处填入一个适当的词语_____。
5. 文中描写男孩目光神情的词语是_____。

3

In July 2001, Zhang Jian, a 37-year-old swimmer landed in Calais, France after swimming for twelve hours. He became the first Chinese ever to cross the English Channel. The 33. 8-kilometre channel has attracted many swimmers because it is one of the most difficult to cross.

Zhang Jian (A) _____ at 1:30 pm (Beijing time) on July 29, 2001. After putting some oil on his skin to help keep warm, he (B)stepped into the sea from Shakespeare Beach, Dover. Most of the time, (C)Zhang swam freestyle to save energy. But he had to change his style along the way because the ocean currents changed every six hours and the water was so cold. During the crossing, he ate some food and had some drinks. About three hours before he landed in Calais, a British guide jumped into the sea and (D)和他一起游泳. At 1:25 am on July 30, 2001, Zhang walked onto the beach at last.

(E)A lot of people were waiting for him on the beach. Among them were his family and friends. They were very proud of him. A foreign reporter spoke highly of him, "He has shown us what is courage and what is strength."

1. 在(A)的空白处填入适当的词语:_____。

2. 写出(B)和(E)的同义词或近义词:_____,_____。(每空一词)

3. 改写(C)句:Zhang swam freestyle _____ _____ he could save energy.

(每空一词)

4. 将(D)译成英语:_____.

5. 在文中找出最能概括文章大意的语句:_____

(2007 沈阳市中考卷)

4

阅读下面短文,根据短文内容,按照事件发生的先后顺序排序(开始句和结尾句序号已给出)。

When Julia Somberg eats her favorite food, she feels bad. She knows that chocolate can have a lot of fat and sugar. But Julia says she loves chocolate so much—once she starts eating it, she can't stop.

Julia isn't the only one who loves chocolate. It is a favorite food for people all over the world. People prefer chocolate over ice cream, cakes, and cookies.

The idea of eating chocolate didn't begin until the 19th century. Before that, people drank chocolate. The habit began in Central America where the Aztecs drank bowls of chocolate to stay watchful. When the liquid(液体)chocolate was brought to Spain in the 1500s, people thought it was medicine because it had a medicine taste. In fact, the people who made chocolate into drinks were doctors.

Then people discovered that mixing chocolate with sugar made a wonderful drink. King Ferdinand of Spain loved this drink so much that he put out an order: anyone who talked about chocolate outside the court(法庭)would be killed. For about 100 years, chocolate was a secret in Spain.

Finally, people found out about chocolate, and it became a popular drink in Europe. Later, the Swiss mixed milk and chocolate. Today, most Americans prefer milk chocolate, while most Europeans prefer dark chocolate.

New research shows that chocolate is actually good for us. "Chocolate has different kinds of vitamins," says a researcher in France. "It has more than 300 different chemicals. One chemical works on the part of the brain(大脑)that feels pleasure. People who feel good when they eat chocolate are actually healthier. Feeling pleasure is important for health and can protect against illness." "Good chocolate doesn't have much fat or sugar. You can enjoy it if you eat a little at a time!" says Tara Berish, another chocolate lover.

_____ Doctors made chocolate into drinks.

__1__ The Aztecs drank chocolate to stay watchful.

_____ Chocolate was a secret in Spain for 100 years.

_____ Liquid chocolate was brought to Spain from Central America.

_____ Sugar was mixed with chocolate to make a sweet drink.

__7__ Research has shown that chocolate is good for us.

_____ The Swiss put milk into the chocolate mixture.

（2007 天津市中考卷）

第三部分　参考答案

第一部分　客观阅读理解

人物类

1 FTFFF　2 FFTTT　3 BCDAB　4 CBDCB　5 CDCCA　6 CDCBD　7 FTTFT　8 CCDCD

9 BCCAB　10 FFTFT　11 CBCDC　12 CACDC　13 CBADB　14 CBDCD　15 CBDAC　16 CADCA

17 DCDBA　18 BACCB　19 ABCCB　20 DCACC

体育类

1 DDBCC　2 BAAAA　3 CCABB　4 TFFTT　5 FTFTT　6 TTFFT　7 TFTFT　8 FTFTF

9 CCBDB　10 BACDD　11 ABACA　12 TFTTF　13 BABCA　14 BDACB　15 CDABB　16 DCCDD

17 BDCDD　18 DCACB　19 DBADB　20 AABDC

科技类

1 FTTTF　2 TFFFT　3 TFTFF　4 DCCAD　5 BABCA　6 ADBCB　7 ADCBA　8 ABDCD

9 DAADC　10 DBCBA　11 BCCAB　12 ABCBB　13 CBBCC　14 TFFTF　15 BDADD　16 ABDCC

17 BDCAD　18 BCADC　19 DADAC　20 CDBAA

应用类

1 ADBAC　2 BBDDA　3 BBBAD　4 ABDCD　5 AABBA　6 CDBCA　7 DACBD　8 CDBCB

9 CDBAB　10 DDACB　11 CACCD　12 ADCDB　13 CBCBA　14 ADCCD

15 BCDAA　16 DADBB　17 BACBD　18 CDBDA　19 CDDBD　20 DCCAD

说明类

1 DBDCC　2 TTTFT　3 FTTFT　4 CDDCD　5 BADCB　6 CACDC　7 TTFTT　8 ACAAB

9 TTFFT　10 TFTTT　11 TFTFF　12 BABAD　13 DCBBC　14 CCABA

15 CDABC　16 CDAAB　17 ADDCB　18 CDBAD　19 BBADC　20 CDCAC

第二部分　主观阅读理解

题型一

1

1. To save his life.

2. 我跑步不但是为了残疾人，而且是为了每一个人。

3. He talked about cancer and being disabled.

4. Five.

5. Nothing is impossible if you put your heart into it. (one possible answer)

2

1. Because television has now come to nearly every family. / Because some children watch TV about twenty hours a week.

2. It helps them learn about their country and the world.

3. There are too many programmes about love and crime on TV，and children simply watch too much television. Some programmes of education don't help children a lot.

4. They need to play in order to learn about the world. They need to do with their parents and friends，and they need to have sports.

5. Children and Television.

3

1. Because the school wanted to test the students' knowledge and morality.

2. Two.

3. Hua Nan thinks if there are no invigilators，some students will cheat. Students won't be able to ask for help when they need. This kind of exams are too early.

4. No-teacher exams.

5. 学校必须信任学生，考试无需监考。

4

1. For Aaron's birthday.

2. No，they didn't.

3. Because Joe/he was ill and couldn't watch the game this time.

4. Yes，he did.

5. C

5

1. A superstar is someone who is unusually famous in sports，films，or popular music.

2. 拳击比赛冠军。

3. Maybe. But maybe they will be forgotten tomorrow.

4. These days Ali is known little by people.

5. 他是体育运动史上最伟大最著名的拳击运动员之一。

6

1. No，it isn't.

2. On December 4th，1619.

3. President Abraham Lincoln.

4. 幸运的是

5. 他们感谢上帝在一年中给他们带来的好事以及好收成。

7

1. Teleshopping is a way to buy the things you know from TV by phone.

2. A number of European countries.

3. In France.

4. Because they can do some shopping at home.

5. Good quality.

8

1. It's when the farmer is getting land ready to grow plants.
2. He has to turn the ground over first.
3. Because there was no machine.
4. They don't need rain.
5. Yes，they do.

9

1. He is living a simple life.
2. He wanted to look for a job.
3. No，he doesn't.
4. No，he doesn't.
5. Because he saw his money was well used and this made him closer to the child.

10

1. It is spread all over the store.
2. The more expensive food is in packages with brightly colored pictures and is placed at eye level so you see it and want to buy it.
3. They can find things on lower shelves.
4. By moving products to eye level.
5. Yes，they do.

题型二

1

1. terrible and with broken buildings and things of that kind
2. Hungry and rude
3. Laughing，friendly and understanding
4. Amazing
5. exactly the same

2

1. Los Angeles
2. sixteen
3. *The Asphalt Jungle*
4. thirty-one films
5. thirty-six

3

1. weather
2. 9:00 am to 5:30 pm
3. parks
4. wait in line
5. right

4

1. in detail/ carefully/ that you'd like to do

2. keep full notes

3. Make a list

4. （more）well-organized

5. the result of your work

5

1. 9 2. out 3. of 4. 1826 5. write

题型三

1

1. fortune 2. cleverest 3. fill 4. candle 5. light

2

1. troublemaker 2. behavior 3. matured 4. leader 5. person

3

1. presenter 2. modern 3. desk 4. write 5. without

4

1. under 2. noise 3. left 4. crossing 5. pockets

5

1. upset 2. not 3. fat 4. unlocked 5. dangerous

其他题型

1

1. atmosphere 2. oxygen 3. carbon dioxide 4. weight/pressure

5. the sun's heat 6. expands/ takes up more space

2

1. went to get a cup of coffee 2. said nothing 3. the last piece

4. under 5. closely, strange

3

1. set off 2. walked Many 3. so that 4. swam together with him

5. He/ Zhang Jian became the first Chinese ever to cross the English Channel.

4

3 1 5 2 4 7 6(包含已给出的1和7的答案序号)

图书在版编目(CIP)数据

中考英语阅读理解专项训练 / 黄侃主编;方星分册主编.—南京:南京大学出版社,2009.6(2009.8 重印)
(英语满分训练)
ISBN 978 - 7 - 305 - 06238 - 4

Ⅰ.中…　Ⅱ.①黄…②方…　Ⅲ.英语－阅读教学－初中－习题－升学参考资料　Ⅳ.G634.415

中国版本图书馆 CIP 数据核字(2009)第 103138 号

出 版 者　南京大学出版社
社　　　址　南京市汉口路 22 号　　　　　邮　编　210093
网　　　址　http://www.NjupCo.com
出 版 人　左　健

丛 书 名　英语满分训练
书　　　名　**中考英语阅读理解专项训练**
总 主 编　黄　侃
分册主编　方　星
责任编辑　顾　越　王　慧　　　　编辑热线　025 - 83592123
照　　　排　南京紫藤制版印务中心
印　　　刷　南京人文印刷厂
开　　　本　787×1092　1/16　印张 8.75　字数 189 千
版　　　次　2009 年 6 月第 1 版　2009 年 8 月第 2 次印刷
ISBN　978 - 7 - 305 - 06238 - 4
定　　　价　15.00 元

发行热线　025 - 83592169　025 - 83592317
电子邮箱　Press@NjupCo.com
　　　　　Sales@NjupCo.com(市场部)